ANNE HAMPSON

dark hills rising

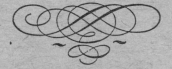

HARLEQUIN BOOKS
toronto·winnipeg

© Anne Hampson 1971

Original hard cover edition published in 1971
by Mills & Boon Limited

SBN 373-70595-6
Harlequin Presents edition published June 1975

Printed in Canada.

CHAPTER ONE

Two graceful white swans glided across the lake, and on the bank ducks and geese preened themselves in the warm February sunshine. The unusual mildness of the temperature had brought office and shop workers into the park and they strolled along the lakeside or took to the grassy rise where snowdrops and crocuses bloomed in profusion beneath the leafless trees.

Gail sat on a bench, a book unopened on her lap. It was her lunch-hour break and for the past twenty minutes she had been enjoying the fresh air, and the flowers and the song of the birds. But all at once she stiffened as two young children came skipping along the path, followed by their parents.

Could she move away unseen? The naked trees and bushes offered no cover at all and Gail sat still, praying she would remain unnoticed.

'Daddy, can we feed the swans?' the small girl, aged four, lifted a pretty face to the smiling man above her; he took a crust of bread from the paper bag in his hand and gave it to her.

'I want some as well.' The boy, three years older than his sister, took the bread offered and threw it into the lake.

'Don't go too near the edge,' warned their mother, a rather plain young woman of about twenty-nine years of age. She stood by the pram, but her eyes were on the children standing on the lakeside.

They were laughing and chattering, but the baby in the pram slept peacefully. A boy . . . born just six weeks ago.

As Gail's eyes moved, to become fixed on the man, she noted with a little sense of shock that his hair was receding, and as he turned to grab hold of one of the children who had strayed too close to the edge, she saw a tiny bald patch on the crown of his head.

But he would be thirty-three now—thirty-four on the tenth of July. . . .

Nine years since it had happened. As always bitterness came with recollection, but the expression in Gail's beautiful brown eyes as she looked at the children was one of yearning, and in her heart there was a dull ache of hopelessness. These lovely children . . . all this could have been hers had not fate decided otherwise.

What could she do? For some considerable time she had been undecided, but now she knew she must have a post where she could be with children. She would change her job, and very soon.

To her dismay the woman had noticed her and was speaking to her husband. He turned, and Gail rose, moving towards the rim of the lake, her eyes on the little girl who was impatiently asking for more bread.

'Gail, how are you? Long time no see!'

'I'm fine, Michael, thank you.' Gail managed a smile, and a friendly nod for Joan. Michael's eyes were on her, taking in the delicate lines of her face, the clear fresh bloom of her skin and the long dark lashes of which he had often spoken so flatteringly. He saw the mass of gleaming chestnut hair, and seemed to be fascinated by the flick of a curl which lay so enchantingly on one delicate blue-veined temple. Gail flushed, knowing he had a mental picture of what lay hidden beneath that lock of hair.

'You're not a day older,' he declared impulsively, and a slight frown touched his young wife's brow. 'How long is it since I last saw you?'

The ghost of a smile appeared on Gail's lips. She knew the date exactly, but she merely said,

'Several years, Michael. You only had Darryl then.' She glanced down, smiling, as the boy raised his head on hearing his name mentioned. The baby moved and Gail bent over the pram. 'What have you called him?'

'You knew we had a boy?' Joan's voice held surprise.

6

'I saw the announcement in the paper.' Gail blinked rapidly, for a heaviness had settled at the back of her eyes.

'We called him William, after Michael's father.'

'He'd be thrilled about that.' How well they had agreed, Michael's father and herself. His son was the luckiest man on earth, William Bankfoot had so often told Gail. He took the break badly and for a long while he and his son were estranged.

'Daddy, I want some more bread.' Tricia tugged at her father's sleeve. 'The swans are swimming away. Be quick!'

Gail glanced at her watch.

'I must go, otherwise I'll be late.'

'Are you still working in the same office?' asked Joan politely.

'Yes, I'm still there.' She turned to Michael. 'Well,' she began awkwardly, 'goodbye.'

'Goodbye, Gail.'

The meeting with her ex-fiancé brought on a state of unrest which continued throughout the afternoon and remained with Gail even when she reached home at six-thirty in the evening. Since the death of her mother she had lived with Beth and Harvey, her sister and brother-in-law, and on entering the house she was greeted with the familiar,

'Hello, Auntie Gail!' from both her sister's children at once.

'Hello, darlings.' A kiss for each and then Gail had to listen to all the day's happenings.

'I've been chosen for the football team,' was Thomas's proud announcement. 'I'm the youngest in the team because I'm not eleven yet.'

'That's wonderful, Thomas, but I knew you'd be chosen.' Taking off her coat, Gail threw it over her arm. 'What about you, Marilyn?'

'I'm the new milk monitor!'

'That's nothing,' said her brother disparagingly. 'It isn't an honour waiting on all those kids.'

7

'I agree, Thomas,' said his mother from the kitchen. 'I certainly shouldn't want the job of handing out bottles of milk to forty little perishers.'

'You horrid Mummy! We're not little perishers!' Marilyn scowled. 'We're nice, well-behaved children.'

'That,' laughed Beth, entering with a tray, 'is a matter of opinion.' Putting down the tray she told the children to run off and play. 'We want a cup of tea in peace.'

They went at once, aware of the time and knowing one word of argument would result in their bedtime being brought forward half an hour or so.

'I saw Michael and Joan today,' said Gail as she sat down opposite to Beth. 'They have a new baby.'

'How very nice for them,' returned Beth in acid tones. 'Does Michael get drunk before taking his family out for a drive in the car?'

Gail ignored that.

'They've called him William, after Michael's father.'

Why couldn't she keep quiet? Beth was colouring angrily, as she always did if Michael's name was mentioned. However, Beth was obviously endeavouring to control her temper because all she said was,

'I know you adore kids, Gail, always have from being quite small yourself. But forget Michael and his children. You're beautiful, and sooner or later someone will——'

'Beautiful?' Gail raised her brows. 'With all these scars?'

'All but one are where they can't be seen. In any case, you've no need to carry them. Surgery has progressed considerably in the past nine years.'

This was true—but although surgery could erase the disfigurements from her body, there was no cure for what Michael had done when he crashed that car.

'You're beautiful,' repeated Beth. 'And you're intelligent. You'll marry, no matter what you insist on saying to the contrary. And when you do marry you'll be very sure you're wanted for yourself alone.'

'I'm twenty-eight,' Gail reminded her, and added bitterly, 'in any case, who would ever want a barren woman?'

A swift frown darkened her sister's face.

'Don't use that word!'

'Is there a more apt one?' Gail's voice was cool, covering her emotion, but her thoughts were with Michael's children, and an intense longing enveloped her. She still had the natural desires of a woman, still yearned for the fulfilment only motherhood can bring. The deep sense of loss, and the finality of the doctor's verdict, were rarely absent from her consciousness. 'No, Beth, there's not the remotest possibility of my marrying.'

'That Michael Bankfoot!' Beth exploded. 'Why did he escape without a scratch? Why wasn't he maimed for life——!'

'Beth!' interrupted Gail, shocked.

'Yes, I know I'm hateful and vindictive, but you're my sister and he's nothing to me. He was drunk and yet he escaped. And to throw you over because you couldn't have children—when it was all his fault!'

'He adores children, Beth, and——'

'So do you! He was utterly wicked to act like he did. And what makes me so furious is the way everything seems to go right for him, while you——' She broke off as her husband's car could be heard coming along the drive. 'You'll find someone, though,' went on Beth with confidence. 'Someone worth a hundred Michael Bankfoots!'

But Gail was shaking her head.

'I should have to warn any man who wanted to marry me, just as I warned Jerry Lathom.'

'Jerry was nice,' reflected Beth. 'You told him too soon, Gail.'

'I don't agree.'

'You could have waited until he was really in love with you. Why, you told him only a month after meeting him.'

9

'Because I saw how things were going. We were falling in love with one another and I knew I must tell him at once, for both our sakes. Had he not minded, our relationship could have taken its course, but he did mind; he wanted a family, which after all is only natural. The break came before either of us cared enough to be seriously hurt. He thanked me for my honesty and I know I did right in telling him just when I did.'

'I suppose so,' Beth agreed reluctantly, adding, 'I've never asked you this, Gail—but do you still feel something for Michael?'

Looking straight at her, Gail shook her head.

'Nothing. Today it was only the children who made me feel—well, unhappy. I know they could never have been mine, but I couldn't help imagining mine would have been rather like them.' She paused in thought. 'No, Beth, Michael killed my love when he threw me over. I'm not able to adopt the role of an understanding, forgiving little heroine. I'm human; he was to blame for what happened and he should never have broken our engagement. However, it was a test; his love didn't stand that test and so I'm destined to remain a spinster.'

Beth sighed impatiently, but said nothing, and a moment later she went into the kitchen to put the finishing touches to the dinner.

Gail went upstairs and a short while later, with her hair tucked up under a waterproof cap, she was preparing to take a bath. The lock of hair was off her temple; the scar stood revealed, dark and ugly against the peach bloom of her skin. The other scars were on her body—two on her thighs and one great gash running from her right shoulder to the centre of her back. Her injuries were multiple and it was a miracle she had lived, the doctors had declared.

Several times she had contemplated entering hospital for the operations which were now possible, but always she had changed her mind. There was no one

10

except herself to see her body, so why take all the trouble?

Gail had a week's holiday due to her from the previous year; she had to take it before the end of March and had planned to spend it with her younger sister, Heather. Heather had married a wealthy man and they had a magnificent house on the edge of Sherwood Forest. Gail visited them at least twice a year and she was now looking forward to the luxury of having her morning tea brought up by the maid, who would then run her bath water and do all the necessary clearing up afterwards.

She went straight from work on thc Friday, and on arrival at the railway station was surprised to be met by the chauffeur, as Heather invariably made a point of meeting Gail herself. However, the chauffeur soon explained. Roger's mother had had a fall and Heather had gone to see what she could do for her.

'I drove your sister there,' he went on, 'and then came to meet you. I'm going to pick her up when I've dropped you at the house.'

'Is Mrs. Swinbourne hurt badly?'

'No. Her housekeeper rang, saying the old lady was shaken, but there didn't appear to be any injuries.'

On arrival at Heather's home Gail was greeted by Trudy, one of the resident maids, who took Gail up to the room she always occupied at the front of the house.

'I'll unpack for you, Miss Kersley,' she offered. 'You go and have some tea. Greta will make it for you.'

'I'm not tired, or thirsty. I'll give you a hand with the unpacking.' She took her toilet requirements into the bathroom and on her return Trudy said,

'We've two children visiting us—so now we've four. They keep us alive, I can tell you. I'm glad they're not staying long.'

'Two children? My sister didn't say anything when I rang her on Tuesday.'

'They didn't arrive until Wednesday evening. Their

11

father's a Scottish laird. He's a friend of Mr. Swinbourne. They went to school together.'

'A Scottish laird——? Ah, yes, the Laird of Dunlochrie.'

'That's right. I forgot you knew him.'

'I don't know him, but my sister's mentioned him once or twice.' Heather disliked him excessively, Gail recalled, saying he was short and abrupt to the point of rudeness. 'Is he not here with his children?'

'No; he has some business to see to in London and Mr. Swinbourne had evidently suggested that he leave the kiddies here. He'll pick them up again on his way back next week.'

'He's a widower, I believe?' Gail took her nightgown from the suitcase and placed it under the bed cover.

'He is, yes.' A small hesitation and then, 'I couldn't help overhearing a little of the conversation on the evening Mr. MacNeill brought them. He said he was going to London to find a nanny for the three children—well, I suppose it's for the three.'

'Three?'

'He has a girl of fifteen, but he left her at home.'

Heather had mentioned only two children, Robbie, seven, and Shena, five and a half.

'What's the elder girl's name?'

'Morag.' Trudy paused. 'There's a very big gap in the ages, isn't there?'

'Between Robbie and Morag? Yes, there is a big gap.' Andrew MacNeill was thirty-seven, Heather had once mentioned. He must have been married quite young if he had a daughter of fifteen.

Trudy lifted the last two sweaters from the case and put them in a drawer. She then closed the case and took it into the dressing-room out of the way.

'That's it, Miss Kersley. Shall I make you some tea now?'

'Please, Trudy. I'll be down directly.'

After washing her face and brushing her hair Gail went down to the sitting-room, and only seconds later

Heather came in, full of apologies for not meeting Gail at the station.

'Grandma's housekeeper rang and said she'd had a fall. I had to go, even though Grandma wasn't badly hurt. I've promised her Roger will go over this evening, so we'll have an hour or two to ourselves.' She stood for a moment, smiling at Gail. There had always been a great affection between the three sisters, although in looks they bore not the slightest resemblance to one another. Heather was fair and pretty, while Beth was dark and somewhat plain. Gail, with her delicate classical features, gave at first glance the impression of fragility, but in character she was in fact the strongest of the three. 'Have you had something to eat?'

'Trudy's making some tea—— Here she is.'

'I've made sandwiches, and the scones are hot. Is there anything else you would like?'

'No, Trudy, this is fine, thank you. Where are the children?' She turned to Gail. 'Has Trudy told you about our visitors?'

Gail nodded.

'They're away in the woods somewhere,' said Trudy, laying down the tray and bringing a small table up to the fire. 'I told them not to go too far. I think they'll do as they're told,' she added with a grimace.

The table set, Trudy went out and Gail immediately asked about the children of the Laird of Dunlochrie.

'They're rather sweet, especially Robbie. It's the father I can't abide,' said Heather.

'He's in London, Trudy says.'

'Yes. Apparently he has difficulties with his nannies——'

'You sound as if he has several.'

'He's had several.' Heather passed Gail her tea and offered the scones. 'I don't know much about him. As I've told you before, he's Roger's friend, not mine. And Roger doesn't talk much, but from what I can gather Andrew's wife was a thorough bad lot, and his elder daughter takes after her. She's the trouble where a

13

nanny is concerned. They never stay—won't stand her arrogance and disobedience.'

'Isn't she a little old for a nanny?'

'The nanny isn't for her, but she's the one who makes their lives unbearable and so they just don't stay. You can't treat servants like that these days or you jolly soon lose them.'

'But Mr. MacNeill is now looking for another nanny?' What was at the back of her mind? Andrew MacNeill would in all probability bring the new nanny back with him in a few days' time.

'He advertised in the London papers—he wants an English girl, apparently. And so he had to go there to interview the applicants. He has a friend who's put his flat at Andrew's disposal.'

Gail stirred her tea, deep in thought.

'There's a big gap between the ages of the children— between the elder girl and Robbie, I mean. Trudy tells me she's fifteen.'

'I don't know the whole story. As I've said, Roger won't talk—loyalty to his friend and all that sort of nonsense. You know what men are,' added Heather, clearly piqued. 'However, I have gathered that Andrew's wife went off with someone else when Morag was three, and she didn't come back for a year.'

'He forgave her?'

'He must have done. I think, basically, he's a good man, and would abide by his promises. Yes, he'd consider marriage to be permanent. Anyway, I suspect he jibbed at having more children just in case he was left again with them, should his wife repeat the performance, which, incidentally, she did. However, the next time she came back they had Robbie; I suppose he decided he wanted an heir, after all. Then eighteen months later Shena was born. Their mother was killed in a skiing accident. She was supposed to be having a holiday with an old school friend, but was on holiday in Austria with one of her boy-friends.'

'*One* of her boy-friends?'

14

'Roger likes to give her illness, as he terms it, a more delicate name, but I'm catty and have an altogether different name for it!' Heather poured another cup of tea and added, 'The daughter takes after her and has given her father no end of trouble.'

'At fifteen!' Gail was shocked.

Heather shrugged. 'They start much earlier than that these days.'

'Poor Mr. MacNeill. How very dreadful for a man in his position to be so disgraced.'

'I don't know,' returned Heather indifferently. 'It's not as if he's a nice sort of person.'

'What's he like?' asked Gail curiously.

'Have I never told you?'

'You've not said much about him. I know he's thirty-seven and a Scottish laird, and that's about all.' Gail smiled to herself. 'You said he invited you to his house but you refused to go because you couldn't stand him.'

'For the deerstalking, yes, I remember. He wanted Roger to go and thought he had better include me. I obligingly refused and Roger went alone.'

'Why don't you like him?'

'He's too arrogant and pompous, for one thing, and I really don't know what Roger sees in him. But Roger becomes quite vexed when I say anything about Andrew, so I keep quiet about the wretched man. I've seen him on only three occasions and each time he's scarcely had the patience to speak to me, and even when he does speak he's so sharp that I feel sure he's a woman-hater.'

'Could be, if he's suffered so much at the hands of his wife and daughter.'

'Can't see him suffering; he's too hard and unfeeling—a typical Scot. I expect it was humiliation more than any real hurt that upset him.'

'But he must have loved his wife to take her back twice.'

'That I wouldn't know. He doesn't seem capable of love as far as I can see.'

15

Gail fell silent for a while, wondering if it were love for his wife or honour of his pledge that had induced him to take his wife back.

'It does seem a shame that this daughter is now causing him this humiliation, for people will know, of course?'

'You can't keep a thing like that secret.' Heather paused and added, 'As I said, I don't know very much about him, but the second time I saw him it was at the home of one of Roger's school friends. Mary, the wife, was a talkative sort of woman and she did tell me what little she knew. There's no doubt that Morag is as wicked as her mother was, being far too fond of the men. She's also dishonest; she stole money from one of her friends and went off abroad somewhere with her young man.'

'She's as bad as that?'

'According to Mary, Morag MacNeill isn't fit to live.' Heather took a scone and buttered it, thoughtful for a while. 'She actually hinted that Morag wasn't his.'

'Not his? But what a thing to say!'

'She came early, but at that time Andrew would naturally trust his wife, and would never suspect her of deception. Whether or not he remains unsuspecting no one will ever know.'

'I don't wonder he's hard and unfeeling,' murmured Gail almost to herself. 'He's really to be pitied.'

'Pitied! He'd not thank you for pity. Wait until you meet him.'

'I shall meet him?'

'He's due back on Wednesday. You're not leaving until Saturday.'

'He has a large estate, I suppose?'

'He wouldn't be a laird unless he had. On the home estate he has many thousands of acres, but he also has other estates, even larger, further north. I believe he has other interests—in industry, I think Roger said. He 's hard, I'll admit that, and he's a terribly im- ~son, being a member of the Queen's bodyguard—the Royal Archers and all that.' She broke off, listening. 'Here come the children. Just hark at that din!'

Eagerly Gail glanced through the window. Racing across the lawn, shouting at the tops of their voices, came the four children; within seconds the door was flung wide and two of them entered the room, flushed and breathless.

'Auntie Gail! How long have you been here?' Manda hugged her and gave her a loud kiss. 'We've got visitors!'

'So I see.'

'Come and shake hands with Auntie Gail,' Manda invited, beckoning to the two standing by the door.

'They're shy,' laughed Simon. 'Come on, Auntie Gail won't eat you!'

'How do you do?' Robbie came first, extending a small, and not very clean, hand.

'I'm pleased to meet you, Robbie.' Gail looked at him. Sturdy and strong, with firm features even at this early age. 'And this is your sister?'

'I'm Shena.' She examined Gail suspiciously before holding out her hand. Neither so warm nor so spontaneous as her brother, Gail decided, and an unaccountable frown touched her brow. 'Are you staying here?'

'For a little while.' The hand was cold, and withdrawn swiftly.

'Come and play with us,' invited Simon. 'Like you always do.'

'Auntie Gail is having her tea.'

Gail did eventually go out and they all played cricket on the lawn. The following day she and Heather took the children to the woods and on the Sunday Roger took them for a drive and they stopped at a little country inn for tea. Manda and Simon had the following two days off school, it being the half-term break, and as the weather remained fine and warm they all spent their time out of doors.

17

'You love it, don't you?' commented Heather in one unguarded moment, and Gail nodded wistfully. She was in her element, but the days went by far too quickly and although in some strange way she was looking forward to meeting the children's father she was sadly regretting this swift passage of time.

He arrived just before dinner on the Wednesday, Roger having met him at the station, for he had left his car in one of Roger's garages and gone to London by train. Gail was upstairs, changing, when she saw the car stop in the drive. She stood by the window as the two men alighted. Tall and upright, with broad powerful shoulders, Andrew MacNeill made an impressive figure. But he had turned towards the house before Gail could examine his features, and she proceeded with her dressing. Taking a last look at herself in the mirror, and making sure the half-fringe was fixed exactly in place, she went downstairs and into the sitting-room where her sister and brother-in-law were having a drink with their guest. Andrew turned as she entered, flicked her an indifferent glance and then continued his conversation with Roger. Not very good manners ... and yet for some reason Gail excused him. Roger smiled and spoke quickly.

Her hand was taken in a grasp that made her wince, but after the brief introduction Andrew lost interest in her. He also practically ignored Heather, who made a face behind his back and invited Gail to help her with the dinner.

'Aren't Trudy and Louise doing it?' Gail asked as they went along the short corridor.

'Yes, but I had to get away. Isn't he just too insufferable!' she exclaimed disgustedly. 'Roger'll be so cross with me, but I'm not pandering to his pompous ill-mannered friends!'

'Has he more like that?' laughed Gail.

'One friend, then,' returned Heather angrily. 'There couldn't possibly be more like him!'

'Perhaps he prefers men's company,' said Gail as they

18

entered the kitchen.

'Perhaps?' Heather raised her brows. 'He definitely does prefer men's company.'

'Are you talking of Mr. MacNeill?' Louise wanted to know, taking the joint from the oven.

'None other, Louise.'

'He's the handsomest man I've ever seen,' was the soulful response. 'Masterful, too, just like the films, if you know what I mean.'

Gail met her sister's glance and they both laughed.

'Louise has fallen for him,' submitted Trudy.

'There's no accounting for tastes,' said Heather crisply. 'How is everything going?'

'Perfectly. I've excelled myself with the sauce. I hope Mr. MacNeill will like it.'

'We have two guests, Louise,' said Heather.

'Sorry,' Louise turned to Gail. 'I hope you will like the sauce, too, Miss Kersley.'

'I'm sure I shall, Louise. I've always said no one makes sauces like you.'

Gail sat opposite to Andrew at dinner and as he afforded her no attention at all she could examine his face without embarrassment. Dark features, harsh and lean, a thrusting jaw and strong firm mouth. His black hair, waving slightly and greying at the temples, was brushed back from a lowering brow; his eyes were dark blue, hawk-like and piercing under thick, straight brows. Fierce he looked, and somehow barbaric. Yet the lines of his face and impressive air instantly stamped him a noble member of the Scottish aristocracy.

Inevitably he sensed her interest at last and turned a mild and arrogantly questioning stare in her direction. She flushed and glanced down at her plate. But she knew his eyes were still on her and involuntarily she touched the hair on her temple. She felt the scar through it and wondered why she should be concerned that it might just be visible.

Much later she gathered from his conversation with

Roger that he had not been successful in his quest for a suitable nanny, and much later still, Heather having gone upstairs and Roger having gone out to garage the car, Gail said a trifle breathlessly,

'My sister tells me you've been advertising for a nanny?'

'That is what I gave her and Roger to understand.' A deep voice, clipped and cool, but Gail scarcely noticed. For his answer was strange, and evasive, but she had no time to speak again because Trudy entered with the supper tray. A few minutes later Heather returned, but there was complete silence in the room until the appearance of Roger.

'Must you go tomorrow?' he asked. 'How about staying for a couple of days?'

Heather's face was a study as she awaited Andrew's reply.

'Thanks, I will.' The voice remained clipped, but it also contained a hint of dejection which was wholly out of character. However, his feelings, whatever they were, became successfully hidden as he began once again to chat with his friend.

From the first Robbie had taken to Gail, but his sister retained that air of suspicion. She was aloof, with a certain pride in her manner which seemed strange in so young a child. Nevertheless, all four children were ready to have Gail play with them and once or twice Gail caught Andrew looking oddly at her. This was very apparent when, one day after tea, Gail sat in the small sitting-room reading to them. They were all on the rug at her feet with Robbie closest to her, his dark curly head resting against her knee. She glanced up to see Andrew standing in the doorway, his gaze fixed intently upon her. She stopped reading, embarrassed that he should be watching her, so silently.

'Oh, please go on, Auntie Gail,' begged Robbie, smiling up into her face. 'It's exciting!'

She returned his smile, wondering that he could

have endeared himself to her in so short a time.

'You like the story?'

'It's a lovely story. No one ever reads to us at home.'

She glanced again at the tall man in the doorway and would have closed her book for a moment or two, but he said quietly,

'Don't let me interrupt, Miss Kersley. The children are clearly absorbed.' And with that he stepped back and softly closed the door.

The following evening she was on the balcony, enjoying a few minutes' solitude before going to bed. She had said her good nights, and her goodbye to Andrew, who was leaving very early in the morning. It was a warm and peaceful atmosphere, with the moon sailing through the clouds and the air soft and still, but Gail was enveloped in a restlessness, a restlessness she knew full well resulted from the knowledge that she had said goodbye to Robbie and Shena for ever, for it was mostly unlikely she would meet them again. Robbie had certainly reached her heart, and she thought that had she been fortunate enough to have had a son of her own she would have asked nothing more than that he could have been like Robbie.

Suddenly she turned, every nerve quivering. Andrew had come from the room behind and was standing there, watching her. She turned again, half expecting him to retire into the room, but he stepped out on to the balcony and stood beside her, tall and straight and rather overpowering.

'It's a beautiful night.' She spoke hastily, feeling the silence must be broken before it became oppressive. 'I came out for a breath of fresh air before going to bed.' He made no comment and she continued with the same haste, 'It looks as if you'll have a good journey tomorrow.'

'Most pleasant, I should say.'

'You have your car here, Heather tells me.'

'I have my car here.'

Why had he come to her? Up till now he had shown

little interest in her—and that only when she was with the children. At all other times he did not spare her even a glance. Why had he come? she asked herself again, and although her heart was beginning to beat abnormally she was totally unprepared for his next words.

'Miss Kersley, I've watched you with my children, and as you know, I've been looking for someone to take care of them.'

'Yes,' she said breathlessly, her spirits soaring. 'You were looking for a nanny.'

A small silence; the moon glided into the mask of cloud and for a while his face was cast into the shadows.

'I want someone to take care of my children.'

She waited. She knew what was coming—or thought she did. The moon reappeared; his face was harsh and set and he remained silent in thought.

'You—you haven't found a suitable nanny f-for them?' What answer must she give him when eventually the question did come? This was what she desired—to be with children, to have them in her care and be able to love them just as if they were her very own. Robbie she loved already, and he had an affection for her, but Shena. . . .

'I wasn't looking for a nanny.'

'Not——?' She stared uncomprehendingly. 'Heather said you'd advertised for one, and that was why you went to London.' Even as she spoke Gail recalled his evasive answer of a couple of nights ago.

'I did advertise for a nanny.' A long pause, and then, 'None of the applicants was suitable for my requirements.'

'I don't understand. You just said you weren't looking for a nanny.' What was the matter with him? He spoke in riddles.

'I'm looking for a wife. But naturally I couldn't advertise for one. I had hoped one of the applicants would prove suitable, but, as I've said, none of them did.' So coolly he spoke, and without the least trace of emotion or embarrassment. For a moment Gail wondered if he had proposed marriage to one of the applicants, but soon decided he had not.

'A wife, Mr. MacNeill?'

'My children are deprived—have been from the day they were born. Nannies are not the answer, even could I get one to stay. I want my children to have a mother.'

Why was he telling her this? she wondered, disappointment flooding over her. Only now did she know her answer would have been given eagerly; she would have accepted the post of nanny without a moment's hesitation.

'I see.' She raised her eyes and in them all her shattered hopes were revealed. 'I thought for a moment— for a moment——' She stopped as a break entered her voice. 'I thought you were going to offer me the post of nanny.'

'You would have accepted?'

She nodded miserably. 'Yes, Mr. MacNeill, I would have accepted.'

He moved, and leant his back against the stone support.

'And if I should ask you to care for them—as their mother?'

Of course; she should have known. And yet she stared speechlessly at him for a moment. But then her pulse started to race. To be a wife and a mother.... This was what she had longed for prior to the accident, what she had been so certain was to be her destiny. And this was what she had never thought to be after the accident had occurred and the doctor's verdict had been so gently given. But to marry a stranger ... surely such an action would be going to the extreme lengths of folly.

'I can't—I mean——' She stopped, uncertain and confused. 'It's impossible, Mr. MacNeill. We don't even know each other.'

'You were willing to accept the post of nanny——'

'Yes,' she interrupted breathlessly, hope rising again.

'Yes, I'll accept willingly.'

'The post I'm offering would be very little different. A business arrangement, but binding—very binding, Miss Kersley. For the sake of my children I must marry.' He waited, but Gail had nothing to say and he continued, 'You probably don't know about my elder daughter, but she was deprived of a mother's love and that deprivation has had disastrous results. She is quite beyond redemption. I shall not have my little ones go the same way.'

'Beyond redemption? How can you say that?'

'I hate to say it, naturally. Nevertheless, it's true. What's to become of her I do not know. I've tried, but a man's influence is not enough. She is lost to me, but Robbie and Shena aren't—at least not yet.'

'And they never will be,' she cried. 'They love you—I can tell they love you dearly.'

'Robbie loves me, that's true, but I'm not so sure of Shena. She's beginning to be a difficult child to approach——' He broke off and when he spoke again his voice was vibrant with emotion. 'Shena must not go the way of her sister!'

Gail thought of what Heather had said—that Morag might not be Andrew's daughter, and as she looked up at him, seeing the fine character lines of his face, she felt that this could be true. Surely no daughter of his could be past redemption. And what a thing to say of a fifteen-year-old child. Could she help Morag? Gail wondered. Could she lead her on to the right path?

It was an hour later when Gail and Andrew entered the house. Heather and Roger had gone to bed and so had the maids. All was silent in the great room lit by one small table-lamp as, taking her hand in his, Andrew said unemotionally,

'It must be at once, Gail, you understand that?'

She nodded, wondering at this state of calm where fears could not intrude.

'Yes, Andrew, I understand.'

CHAPTER TWO

HEATHER paced the floor of her sister's room, her face white and strained.

'You're out of your mind, Gail. This obsession for children has affected your brain!'

'I'll be a wife and a mother. Surely you wouldn't deny me that?'

'You'll be neither. You're just deluding yourself. He's said it's to be nothing more than a business arrangement, so how can you be a wife?'

'Sex isn't everything——'

'You're normal; you'll meet someone who'll love you and give you the relationship which is natural. No one ever made a success of the sort of unnatural partnership you're contemplating.' She stopped by the chair where Gail was sitting, and looked down at her pleadingly. 'Think—for heaven's sake, think!'

'I've given him my answer, and I'm not going back on it.'

'You'd like to?' Heather seized on that, but Gail was shaking her head.

'I want to marry him,' she said simply.

Heather threw out her hands.

'You've seen what sort of man he is! He's hard and cruel!'

'Cruel?'

'Where are your eyes? Can't you read his face? And he doesn't like women, you've had proof in plenty of that during the past couple of days. Why, he hasn't the patience to speak to either of us.'

'It's of no importance that he doesn't like women. I'll only be there to look after the children. I don't suppose I'll come into contact with him all that often.'

'Not come into contact with your husband? What a life!'

Gail shrugged.

'You know the position. I've explained it all to you. I'll be his wife—and I want to be a wife, Heather, just like any other woman—but we won't be making demands on one another. That's the only difference.'

'You'll be satisfied with an existence like that?'

'The step I'm taking is of my own choosing. I know exactly what to expect.'

'Business arrangement or not, the fact that he hates women is bound to affect you.'

'It's understandable that he doesn't like women,' returned Gail, veering the trend of conversation away from anything too personal.

'I give up! You'll not be making excuses for him a month from now!'

'A month?' Gail had to smile. 'You're not giving us very long.'

'He'll show you what he is immediately he gets you in his clutches.'

'Heather,' said Gail gently, 'don't be melodramatic.'

'How can a sensible, level-headed girl like you put her head in a noose without even a moment's consideration? Gail, you can't do this!'

'What can he do to me? He's an honourable man and I trust his word. All he wants is a mother for his children, and therefore he'll naturally treat me in a friendly way. As for anything else—well, he was perfectly frank and I accepted the proposal. In any case, we're strangers; a closer relationship would be immoral.'

'You have some very odd ideas. But don't come to me when you discover you've made a complete hash of your life!' Heather began pacing the floor again. 'Beth won't believe it!'

'I'm old enough to shape my own life. I can love those children and if I can help Morag so much the better. I won't have wasted my life, Heather, and as things are now I feel it's being wasted. I can foresee nothing—nothing at all. Perhaps it's difficult for you to

26

understand, because you have Roger and the children, but mine would be a very lonely future were I not to marry Andrew. No, I've made the right decision, and have no qualms at all.'

'Do you really feel you can help that girl when you've said her own father declares her to be past redemption?' Heather looked at Gail and shook her head. 'Would a man like Andrew admit defeat unless he was fully convinced he was defeated?'

Gail frowned and said after a while,

'With regard to that I must agree he doesn't strike me as a man who would. Nevertheless, I can try.'

Heather glared at her.

'Why should you? She's her mother's daughter, and I've told you what Mary said. The girl isn't fit to live!'

'That's a strong statement, Heather. No one is as wicked as that.'

'Everyone can't be wrong. Are you saying her own father exaggerates?'

Gail turned away, her face white, her eyes clouded.

'I can try,' she said stubbornly at last.

'You'll fail.'

'Perhaps. But there are the other two. I can bring them up in the right way, so that Andrew can be proud of them. That will make up in some measure for Morag.'

'These heroics!'

Gail looked at her. Heather was furiously angry and saying things she would never have uttered in ordinary circumstances. But her anxiety was all for Gail—she was far more afraid than was Gail herself. In fact, Gail knew no fears at all. Some strange instinct told her she had chosen the right path, and she trusted that instinct.

'I'm not heroic, as I told Beth a short while ago. No, I'm very human and this step is as much for my own benefit as for the children's. This is the only way I can be a mother; the opportunity came to me right out of the blue and I'd be a fool to cast it aside.'

'If only I could put the clock back—you'd never have met him!'

'We all would like to put the clock back,' returned Gail significantly. 'But that is something none of us can do. I *have* met Andrew, and I intend to marry him, no matter what any of you say.'

'Beth and Harvey will have plenty to say, I warn you of that.'

And they did. Gail went through it all again the following day when she went home to collect her belongings. Roger drove her, the only one of her relatives who had said no word of dissuasion.

'You've only to wait,' Beth argued, 'and you'll have someone who'll love you.' She could lead a normal life, Beth went on, and she and her husband could adopt children. But although the matter was not allowed to rest for one single moment while she packed her things, Gail remained adamant. Yet she did at times wonder at her composure. She visualized no flaws or difficulties. The children would be hers; Andrew would not interfere so long as she did all that was right. He wanted nothing more from her and she did not wish it otherwise. She would run his home, of course, just as any real wife should. He would expect that of her, naturally. No, Gail could see no flaws in the arrangement, and to the disgust of all except Roger she married Andrew the following Tuesday and later the same day they left in the car for his estate in Perthshire.

He did not speak much on the way and neither did Shena. Several times Gail tried to draw her out, but she remained distant. Robbie on the other hand was delighted, finding no difficulty in calling her Mummy, in obedience to her father's order. Shena seemed absolutely determined not to do so, but Gail was not unduly troubled by this; her optimism was such that she felt confident of winning the child over in the not too distant future.

'Have you been in Edinburgh before?' inquired

Andrew as they entered the capital.

'When I was small. We came to Scotland for a holiday.' With a shock she realized she had no idea where her husband lived. 'Is your home far from here?'

'We live in the Highlands,' Robbie informed her at once. 'But we have another house a long way off, don't we, Daddy?'

'Yes, Robbie. It's a hunting lodge,' he then told Gail.

'But it's big,' said Robbie.

'Yes, it's big.'

They were passing through the city; the famous castle was outlined against the sky, the castle where Mary, Queen of Scots gave birth to the king who was to unite the thrones of England and Scotland.

'What do you shoot?' Gail wanted to know.

'Deer.'

'I'm going to shoot them when I'm big.' Robbie leant forward over the back of his father's seat. 'You wouldn't take us with you before when you went shooting, but can we come with you now we've got a mummy?'

'Perhaps. I'll think about it later.'

'Will Mummy shoot?'

'No, Robbie, I will not.'

'She wouldn't be a good enough shot.' Andrew stopped at the traffic lights, but they changed almost immediately and he edged forward again, following a long line of traffic.

'It seems a shame to shoot them.' Gail spoke frowningly, thinking of the beautiful red deer she had seen in the zoo.

'It's part of our way of life,' he said. 'You'll get used to it.' He turned his head for a second, and noticing her expression he added, 'Culling is necessary for the good of the animals themselves. Were they all allowed to live and multiply they would eventually starve. Also, I allow only marksmen on my land, if that's any consolation to you.'

29

'But one could miss,' she said frowning.

'One had better not,' came the grim rejoinder as Andrew pulled up once more behind a line of traffic.

'You mean, the animal is always killed outright?'

'If it isn't then the man responsible must follow it, however long it takes, and then make sure he does kill it. However, as I've said, I allow only marksmen on my land. We never shoot unless we're sure of a swift kill.'

Gail allowed the matter to drop; it still seemed wrong to kill the deer, even though Andrew had explained that it was necessary to do so for the good of the animals themselves.

They crossed the magnificent Forth Bridge, proceeding up through the Ochils, heading northwards all the while towards the Highlands. As they reached Perth, ancient capital of Scotland, Gail's thoughts wandered to such people as Robert Bruce and Montrose, John Knox and the brave and handsome Stuart Prince. So many famous names were associated with the city immortalized by Sir Walter Scott with his great novel, *The Fair Maid of Perth*.

After stopping in Perth for refreshments Andrew surprised Gail by making a detour so that she could see the view from Kinnoul, a spur of the Siddlaw Hills.

'We came once before, didn't we?' Shena, silent for so long, spoke to her father, at the same time putting her small hand in his. 'Can't you see a long way?'

Beyond the wide green valley of the Tay rose the hills, the Ochils through which they had driven, with the Bens to the west and the mighty Grampians to the north.

'It's a fantastic view,' breathed Gail, feeling excited about the new life upon which she was entering, and still enveloped in that sublime state of optimism for the future. She looked down. Robbie's hand was in hers, warm and small, and somehow conveying his affection for her.

They made their way to the car again and were soon

taking the historical road familiar to Bonnie Prince Charlie and his Highlanders, following the valleys of the Tay and Tummel up to Pitlochry, almost in the heart of Scotland. The mountains rose to a clear but darkening sky; the quartzite summit of Mount Schiehallon, touched by the rays of the lowering sun, changed from dazzling white to milky pearl and then to a soft rosy pink. The road wound and climbed, with the massif of Ben Vrakie on their right and the famous Pass of Killiecrankie just ahead. It was an awe-inspiring landscape of grey-capped mountains, wild and lonely heather moors and pine-clad foothills. Ahead rose the heights of Ben-y-Gloe, the Mountain of the Mist, and just to the north-east was the River Tilt, tributary of the Garry. It ran through Glen Tilt, one of the most beautiful glens in the whole of Scotland.

At last Andrew turned off the main road; they climbed steeply, coming to a high wrought-iron gateway flanked by massive stone towers, below which stood the lodges, one either side of the gateway. The mile-long drive, with a bubbling burn running alongsaid it, was bordered by pine trees and larches, with primroses and sorrel clustered round their bases. Blackface sheep grazed on the hillsides, with highland cattle in the distance, merging with the shadowing landscape.

Sweeping lawns surrounded the house, above whose door was the crest of the Clan MacNeill, chiselled into a sandstone plaque.

Andrew swung the car on to the forecourt and his factor appeared from out of the gloom.

'You had a good journey, sir?'

'Very pleasant, thank you, Sinclair.' Andrew slid from the car as Sinclair opened the door at Gail's side, faint surprise on his tough-skinned, deeply-lined face. The children ran off towards the front door as Andrew said, as imperturbably as if he were remarking on the weather,

'Meet my wife. Gail, my estate manager.'

'Your——?' Sinclair made a swift recovery, extending a hand. 'Pleased to meet you, Mrs. MacNeill,' he said, giving her a wooden stare. 'You've brought beautiful weather with you.'

'Thank you.' She laughed, amused. 'It's nice of you to say so, but I suspect you've had the mildest winter for years up here.'

'True, madam. We've had only autumn and spring.'

'Up till now.' Andrew reached into the car to take a briefcase from the shelf under the dashboard. 'We could still have our winter, so don't be carried away by optimism.'

Servants appeared as they entered the great antler-hung hall; more introductions were made and more expressions of welcome were accompanied by wooden stares.

'Gossip will be rife for the next hour or so,' remarked Andrew calmly. 'Marie, show Mrs. MacNeill up to her room, please.'

The room was next to Andrew's, and Gail wondered if anyone had slept in it since Andrew's late wife. She supposed not, and somehow she had no desire to sleep in it herself. But she could not very well tell her husband this. How little she knew of him, the noble Laird of Dunlochrie. And she supposed all she ever would know would be superficial, it being most unlikely the day would come when he would take her into his confidence.

'You like the view, madam?' Marie was middle-aged, dark and smiling. Her accent was decidedly pleasant.

'It's wonderful. Leave my things for the time being, please. I'd like to be alone.'

'Certainly, madam.'

Gail looked out on to the mountains and moors, bathed now in shadows and tinted with crimson and ochre by the last dying rays of the sun. She could just make out a tumbling burn and a loch; closer too a backcloth of pines sheltered the terraced garden and over to the right of the house a swimming pool could be seen.

She turned into the massive room; it was pleasantly warm, being centrally heated, as was the rest of the house. Off the bedroom was a modern bathroom, also a dressing-room. Cream satin curtains reached the floor; on the colourful Persian carpet stood magnificent Queen Anne furniture and in one corner, standing on an inlaid mother-of-pearl table, was an exquisite Chelsea group. As she remained there, pensively looking all around, the full impact of what she had done was felt for the first time. Was all this splendour really for her? Could it be a dream?—or was she really married? Her eyes wandered to the great oaken door, studded and trimmed with ornate wrought-iron hinges and handle. Rising, she tried it. Locked. She stooped down; no key in the other side. The servants would talk, of course, and the truth might just reach Andrew's friends.

A soft knock on the outer door brought her over to it.

'Dinner will be served in one hour, madam,' the young girl informed her, smiling.

'Thank you.' The girl smiled again and walked away.

What was she supposed to do? Gail wondered. Her main duty was to see to the children, but they had disappeared immediately they entered the house. What time did they go to bed? And would they want supper—or did one of the maids see to that?

Should she go down to Andrew for her instructions? It was the only thing to do, but as she opened the door she heard him moving about in the next room.

Hesitating a moment, she knocked.

'Yes?' sharply, and impatiently, or so it seemed to Gail.

'I was wondering what to do. Must I get the children ready for bed?'

He tried the door.

'Is the key there?'

'No.'

33

'Then come round.'

She did as he asked; his door was ajar and she knocked and entered.

'I felt I should be seeing to the children,' she began, a nervousness descending on her for the first time since her unhesitating decision to marry him.

'Normally you'll give them their tea—much earlier than this, of course—and put them to bed. But tonight one of the girls will be doing it, as usual, for I've been without a nanny for some weeks.' He looked at her searchingly. 'Is your room all right?'

Why was he looking at her like that? she wondered. Did she appear tired—or——? Instinctively she put up a hand to her head. No, the scar was not visible.

'It's very nice, thank you.'

'It hasn't been used since my grandmother's day,' he said, as if sensing her thoughts. 'I renovated this wing, and moved in here, only last year.' Gail said nothing and he continued, 'You must be comfortable, Gail, so if there's anything you want you've only to ask.'

'I will; thank you.'

He made to close the door; it was a gesture of dismissal and she went back to her room. It seemed pleasanter now and she had to smile to herself. But she supposed it was natural not to want to use the room occupied by his late wife.

Morag was away visiting friends and Gail had only Andrew for company as she dined with him in a room far too large for cosiness. Slowly a sense of unreality possessed her; this was like a dream from which she must soon awake. The stranger sitting there, his dark face harsh and set in the candle glow, the rather dour-faced manservant waiting on them ... and the silence. Yes, it was the silence more than anything which took away any tangible reality from the situation. Here she was, a new bride, facing a husband who had neither the inclination nor the patience to converse with her.

For Gail the meal was a strain, lasting an unconscionable length of time.

'We'll take coffee in the lounge,' were the only words Andrew spoke when at last the meal did come to an end.

The lounge was a beautiful room, with a great stone fireplace in which logs were burning, showering the whole place with warmth. The lower half of the walls was panelled in oak while on the upper half exquisite tapestries and paintings hung beneath a ceiling beautifully decorated with cherubs and flowers and birds.

Andrew picked up a magazine, while Gail just sat there, feeling rather lonely and lost. Had she acted too impulsively? Should she have listened to her sisters' advice?—stopped to think, and tried to visualize what her life would be like? Surely no woman had ever taken such a step as she with less regard for the future. Heather had asserted that she was making a hash of her life. Would her words eventually prove to be correct?

'I think I'll go up to my room,' she said immediately on finishing her coffee.

He glanced at the clock.

'It's early, but I expect you're tired after the journey.'

'I am, a little.' Awkwardly she rose and, bidding him good night, left him sitting there, reading his magazine.

A wife and a mother....

Gail stood on the hillside, her hair blowing in the wind, her gaze pensive and a little afraid. It was a month since her arrival at Dunlochrie House and she was still as complete a stranger to her husband as on that first evening. A wife and a mother. Heather had said she'd be neither—and it would seem that Heather was right.

True, Robbie was now very close to her, but Shena was, as her father had said, a difficult child, and she remained cool and withdrawn. And as for Morag....

A bitter curve of Gail's lips revealed her thoughts.

35

Morag hated her and made not the slightest effort to conceal that hatred. Nor did she show any respect for her stepmother; before the servants she derided her, declaring outright that her father had married for convenience and that there was not even friendship between him and Gail. Yet strangely Gail had not lost the respect of the servants; on the contrary, they had become warm and understanding, and many small things were done to make her path a little more pleasant.

Of Morag she had been warned, but Gail was totally unprepared for Andrew's mother-in-law who, naturally having access to the house in order to see her grandchildren, visited them at least once a week. Tall and angular, with hard features and jet black hair, Mrs. Davis was a formidable and thoroughly objectionable specimen of womanhood. On every possible occasion she demonstrated her dislike of Gail and Gail did wonder just how long it would be before she was driven to retaliation. She hated trouble, being of a placid disposition, but she did have a temper which, though kept for the most part firmly controlled, certainly made itself felt when on occasions it was aroused.

'How long have you known Andrew?' had been Mrs. Davis's first question when, after a brief introduction, her son-in-law had left them together, only two days after her arrival.

'Not very long,' had been the evasive reply.

'How long?' Dark arrogant eyes raked Gail contemptuously.

Gail looked straight at her, cheeks burning.

'I had known him only a few days when I consented to marry him.'

'So it was his money and position, obviously.'

'I married Andrew, Mrs. Davis, because he asked me to, and because I personally believed I would be able to help his children.'

'My daughter's children!' There was nothing to say

36

to this and Gail remained silent. 'And are you able to help the children?'

'I've only just arrived here. Time alone will prove whether or not I'm good for Robbie and Shena.'

'And Morag?' A faint sneer hovered on the thin hard mouth. 'What are you expecting to do with her?'

'Morag is difficult, but I hope we'll eventually be friends.'

That was a month ago, and already Gail was admitting the truth of Andrew's statement that Morag was beyond redemption.

The girl suddenly came into view over a low rise; she was astride a beautiful horse, handling it with ease and skill as she came down the rise, her golden hair streaming behind her, long and untidy and not very clean. Instinctively Gail put up a hand, patting into place her own hair which had blown away from her forehead, revealing the scar.

The girl halted, but remained astride the horse. Arrogant she looked, and lawless, her face flushed and somehow giving the impression that it had not received a wash that day.

'And how is my new stepmother this afternoon?' she sneered, faint humour in her eyes.

'I'm well, thank you, Morag,' replied Gail with dignity.

The girl's face darkened.

'Quite the lady, aren't we! Little jumped-up wife of the Laird of Dunlochric!'

Carried on the west wind came the pungent smell of burning heather and Gail glanced across to watch for a second or so the thick pall of smoke rising against the clear blue of the sky. Andrew's gamekeeper was destroying the old heather in order to encourage new growth, for only in this way could the grouse be kept on his moors.

Gail turned again, and looked up at Morag.

'Tell me,' she said quietly, 'what satisfaction does it give you to adopt this insolent way with me? We could

37

be friends, you know.'

'Friends with *you*?' The girl's fair brows shot up. So different in colouring from her grandmother—and yet how alike in features. Although decidedly beautiful now, Morag possessed the sort of bone structure which would eventually rob her of this beauty and give to her face the coldness so strongly portrayed in the features of her grandmother. 'I'm not that hard up for friends, thank you very much!' Nimbly she sprang from the horse as a Land-Rover appeared round the bend of the road which wound its way through the vast estate. 'Sinclair, tell someone to take Rusty away.'

'Certainly, miss.' The Land-Rover scarcely slowed down; it was almost immediately lost to view round another bend in the road.

Morag's eyes followed until it was out of sight, her lips drawn back in a snarl.

'That insolent man will hear from me later!' Without a glance at Gail she strode away, down the hill and along the path towards the house.

Gail followed slowly, a sinking feeling in the pit of her stomach. What was to become of the girl? Her insolence to everyone at home, her type of friends, her way of life. . . . Gail had tried hard and had she made the smallest degree of headway she would have persevered, but Gail had already admitted defeat where Morag was concerned.

How Andrew must be suffering. To have a child turn out as Morag was doing must cause an ever-present concern. Gail brought the girl's face into her mental vision. Not a single line to stamp her as Andrew's daughter. But quite often children differed in looks from their parents, so there was nothing definite on which to base the idea that Andrew was not her father.

On reaching the house Gail heard raised voices coming from the sitting-room and she stood for a moment, listening.

'I'll speak to Sinclair in any way I like!' Morag was shouting. 'He's only a servant and should know his place!'

'You'll treat the servants with the same respect they extend to you——'

'They never treat me with respect——'

'Don't interrupt when I'm speaking!' Andrew's voice rasped, harsh and threatening. 'Take care, Morag, because I'm just about ready to send you away.'

A derisive laugh rang out.

'Where to? A boarding school? I've got myself expelled from two already and it wouldn't take me long to do the same again. I'm not being imprisoned, not for you or anyone else. Is it your platonic, upstart little wife who wants me out of the way——?' The voice was quietened abruptly and, wincing as if it were she herself who had been struck, Gail opened the door.

'Andrew—please——' She stopped, almost cowering under his wrathful, astounded gaze. Morag had a hand to her face, but the red marks of Andrew's fingers were not entirely covered. 'Can—can I speak to Morag?'

'Get out!' he thundered. 'Get out and mind your own business!'

Trembling from head to foot, Gail made her way upstairs. She had realized her mistake even as her first words were uttered. Strong as was his personality Andrew could do nothing with Morag; the bitter humiliation resulting from this was to be suffered in secret and that anyone else should witness it must assuredly infuriate him. And that he was infuriated with her Gail very soon discovered. A few minutes later her door was flung wide open and he strode into the room, his face dark with anger, his eyes glinting like points of blue ice as he fixed his gaze upon her.

'Andrew,' she faltered, involuntarily stepping back, 'I'm sorry. I know I shouldn't have interfered, but——'

'Don't you ever dare do so again.' His voice was like the flick of a whip. 'When I require your help or advice I'll ask for it. Until then—know your place, *and keep it!*'

'Yes ... I'm sorry,' she said again, her voice low and unsteady. 'I just thought—thought I might b-be able to help.'

'As I've said, when I need your help I'll ask for it. Have I made myself clear?'

Gail nodded unhappily, but no words left her lips. She caught sight of herself in the mirror; her face was as white as her blouse.

The door closed and she sank down on the bed, a hand to her heart. It raced uncomfortably and she leant back against the pillows, pushing her hair from her clammy brow. She felt the scar, knew it would be livid and raised, as it always was if she happened to be under the influence of some strong emotion.

Her mind was naturally occupied with the scene just enacted. This almost savage being was her husband, the man she had consented to marry only a few days after their first meeting. Eagerly and optimistically she had made vows and promises without any contemplation of future difficulties or regrets. But now Gail wondered if she could go on like this for the rest of her life. The coldness of her husband, the hatred of Morag and open hostility of her grandmother, the withdrawal of Shena. ...

If she must leave it were better to do it now—— But no, she could not subject Andrew to any further humiliation. Besides, Robbie loved her, and needed her. She would not accept defeat so easily; she would stay, and do the work she intended doing. Robbie would make life bearable for her, and even Shena would come round in the end, for she was neither naughty nor intractable. Gail felt that sooner or later the child would respond to patience and love.

Rising after a while, Gail brushed her hair back into place. There was a little time before she had to pick up the children from school and she went into Pitlochry to do some shopping, taking the small car standing beside the Mercedes and the more modest runabout which Sinclair often used. She bought herself a sweater and a fine

40

tweed skirt. Spring flowers in a shop window tempted her and she bought herself a large bunch, which she put on the seat beside her, and as she repeatedly glanced at them on her way to school her spirits lightened. Flowers had always done something for her and with flowers in a room she could never be really unhappy.

The children bounded out of school and got into the back seat of the car.

'Look what I've made!' Robbie displayed his Easter card with pride. 'I've written on it "For Mummy and Daddy". The teacher told me to.'

'That's lovely.' Warmth enveloped her as she took the card and examined it, reading the neatly written words inside. 'Have you not made one, Shena?'

'Mine isn't finished,' replied Shena quietly. 'The paint wasn't dry, so we had to leave them.'

'She puts too much paint on, that's why,' said Robbie. 'I used to do that when I was small. All the babies use too much paint.'

'I'm not a baby!'

'You're in the babies' class, so you must be.'

'Shena is in the first class, Robbie,' said Gail in gentle tones as she started up the car. 'But she is not a baby.'

'I'm six in a little while.'

'A long while,' argued Robbie. 'Your birthday's in July, and that's not till we break up for our summer holiday.'

Shena fell silent; this unwillingness to argue was not natural in a child of her age and Gail spent the rest of the journey trying to draw her out. She failed, and a frown clouded her brow for a while. But she must be patient. Even Andrew had declared Shena to be difficult.

Still clad in her jodhpurs, Morag was sitting on one of the wide steps as Gail drove on to the forecourt and stopped the car. Both children ran off towards the swings on the lawn and Gail took out her parcels. She picked up the flowers—irises and tulips and daffodils—and looked at them for a moment.

'Who bought you those?' demanded Morag pertly as Gail made to pass her on her way into the house.

'I bought them myself.' Stopping, Gail smiled at the girl. 'Would you like some?'

Morag's insolent glance flicked Gail from head to foot.

'Don't be so magnanimous. We've three greenhouses full of flowers much better than those ridiculous little blooms.'

'The blooms are not particularly small,' Gail remarked patiently, touching one pink and yellow tulip with loving fingers.

'If they're what you're used to,' Morag shrugged. 'Father wouldn't give them house room. He never tolerates anything inferior.'

'Well, if I don't compare them I shan't consider them inferior, shall I?'

'Compare them with what?'

'The beautiful blooms in the greenhouse, of course.' The girl threw her another insolent look.

'Someone bought them for you,' she declared, and stood up, coming very close. 'If you wanted flowers you could have cut as many as you liked from the greenhouse—so it's obvious someone bought them for you.' She paused, but Gail remained silent, her mouth compressed. 'Who is he? Is he handsome? And is he a Scot? I prefer Englishmen myself; they're more—er—warm, if you know what I mean——' She broke off, laughing loudly at Gail's shocked expression. 'Perhaps you wouldn't know anything about comparisons there—not having been made love to by a Scot—or at least, not by your Scottish husband.'

'You're disgusting! Aren't you thoroughly ashamed of yourself?'

'Why should I be? I'm not married, whereas you, even if you are a wife in name only——'

'You don't know that, Morag, so please do not refer

to it again!'

The big eyes opened very wide.

'The door, Mrs. MacNeill, has never been opened since you came.'

'You go into my room?' Gail stared at her angrily.

'I like to know what's going on,' replied Morag unashamedly. 'That key was lost years ago and has never been replaced. Of course, Father could come round, if he were so inclined—but he isn't.' Gail said nothing, merely looking at her with disgust, and Morag went on, continuing what she was about to say when Gail interrupted her. 'Even if you are a wife in name only you've no right to be receiving presents from some other man. Ashamed of myself? I like that! You're the one who should be ashamed of yourself—letting another man buy you flowers.' The last words were spoken in a voice deliberately raised; they were also unnecessary, their having been said, in practically the same vein, only a few moments previously. Morag was staring beyond Gail, and Gail turned, her flesh tingling unaccountably. Andrew stood just a few yards away.

'I've already told you, I bought the flowers myself.' But an uncontrollable hint of colour fused her cheeks; Andrew could not help but notice and a sudden frown settled on his harsh set features. He followed Gail into the hall.

'We have flowers in the greenhouse,' he commented, watching her closely. Was he thinking about his late wife?—and wondering if history could possibly be repeating itself?

'I know, Andrew, and had I thought about it I'd have waited until I got home, but I saw these in a shop—and wanted them right away.' Her explanation sounded weak, even to her own ears and she bit her lip. 'It's called impulse buying, I think. They looked so beautiful, and I put them on the front seat, so I could see them all the time.'

She felt silly, and her flush deepened. So did her

husband's frown, but his tones were quiet enough as he said,

'If you want to buy flowers, Gail, then by all means do so. However, we grow enough for our needs and the obvious thing is to use them.'

Something hard was stuck in her throat. He had softened a little, seeming to have forgotten that scene which was indirectly responsible for her buying the flowers, and Gail had an almost irrepressible urge to talk to him like a real wife, to explain her unhappiness, and to let him know she had been a little scared of the future, and that the flowers had helped to restore her spirits again. But she could not, because they were strangers still, and so she murmured something about not buying flowers again, but using those which were grown for the specific purpose of house decoration.

'It was a silly whim on my part,' she went on, lifting her eyes to his, all unconscious of their brightness, or of the quivering movement of her lips. 'I can't explain, though—explain why I bought them, I mean,' she added in answer to the interrogating look he gave her. And, as she remembered Morag's saying he would not give them house room, 'Can I put them in the lounge?'

'Of course you can put them in the lounge.' His frown reappeared. 'You don't have to ask me that, Gail.'

She smiled then, and her doubts fled. She found herself humming a little tune as she went along the hall towards the little store room just off it, where she would find a vase for her flowers.

CHAPTER THREE

ROBBIE and Shena were racing on in front; Andrew and Gail followed at a more leisurely pace. It was Sunday afternoon, and the first occasion on which Andrew had accompanied Gail when she had taken the children out for a walk.

'I'll come with you,' he had said, much to the delight of the children, and much to the surprise of Gail.

'Ooh, Daddy, that'll be fun!' exclaimed Robbie, lifting a rosy-cheeked face and bestowing a happy smile— which was also a 'thank you'—on his father.

'I like my daddy to come with us.' Shena spoke to Gail, and smiled at her. The child was still in that peculiar state of withdrawal and doubt, but gradually Gail was breaking it down. The difference in the personalities of the two children was a source of great interest to her, for no such marked difference existed in either of her sisters' children. Robbie was spontaneous and warm, enthusiastically falling in with everything Gail planned for their amusement. He trusted her implicitly, considering everything she did to be right. 'That'll be fun!' was one of his favourite expressions, and indeed everything was fun to him. Shena on the other hand was far more retiring and cautious. She did not wholly trust Gail, and always appeared reluctant to accompany her and Robbie on their rambles down the glens or on the heathered grouse moors. It was only at bedtime that Gail felt sure of the child, sensing a warmth about her which was kept hidden during the rest of the day. Gail always read to them after seeing to their baths and supper, and at this time she knew a wonderful tranquillity and sense of fulfilment. She experienced the real pleasure of being a mother.

'Please read some more,' Robbie would beg, and his sister would add,

'Yes, *please* read some more.'

And the real sign of victory appeared to come one evening when Shena called her back as she left the room where the child slept.

'Mummy....'

Gail turned, her heart overflowing with thankfulness.

'Yes, darling?'

'I'm not tucked in—because I moved.'

'Then I must tuck you in again, mustn't I?'

Shena remained silent for a while, gazing up at her with those big blue eyes that were so like Andrew's.

'Are you my mummy?'

A small hesitation and then,

'I'm not your real mummy, Shena, you know that, don't you?'

'Yes.' She paused a while. 'Daddy's told me many times that I must call you Mummy, but I didn't like to at first, but now I want to, just like Robbie.'

Bending down, Gail kissed her, unable to voice words. The struggle was over, she thought ... but soon realized her mistake. Although from then on Shena found it easy to address her as Mummy, she could still become withdrawn at times, and uncooperative, and Gail knew she must continue to tread warily, to practise extreme patience and understanding if she were to succeed in her desires.

'Robbie!' Andrew's voice brought Gail back with a start from her musings. Robbie had decided to climb a tree. 'Down—at once!'

Robbie obeyed, jumping from the low branch and waiting for them to reach him.

'I wouldn't have fallen,' he asserted good-humouredly.

'Perhaps not, but you're too small to be climbing trees'.

'Mummy might let me climb when you're not there.' He grinned mischievously up at Andrew, and as Gail glanced from one to the other she took in the likeness

46

of the features. Even at this early age Robbie possessed the firm and noble lines portrayed in his father's face. He had the same dark hair and blue eyes, and although he was as yet not so mercurial in temperament as Andrew, he did possess certain characteristics which, as with Andrew, gave evidence of the old tradition of Scottish lawlessness.

'I shall do nothing of the kind,' returned Gail inexorably.

'All right,' with obliging good humour. 'I'll wait till I'm big.'

They had been strolling just above the road—a road which was very necessary where such vast tracts of moorland had to be traversed—but now Andrew turned and they were making for the beautiful little Loch Charrag, fringed with birch trees, their slender trunks gleaming in the brilliant sunshine, their branches heavy with swollen buds. Away on a rise a herd of roe deer grazed—two bucks with velvet-covered antlers reaching their full new growth, and several graceful does with their young. A pair of buzzards swooped and planed above the herd, but it was the vicious hooded crows that seemed bent on disturbing it. They called raucously and flapped their wings in flight, maliciously endeavouring to scare the cudding deer. But the deer merely looked up now and then, chewing rhythmically. It was only the weak or aged animal who had anything to fear from the hoodies, who would peck out a creature's eyes even while it was still alive.

'Hoodies, Daddy,' cried Robbie. 'Aren't you going to shoot them?'

'Without a gun?'

'You should have brought it; we don't want the hoodies.' Even as he spoke a shot rang out from far down below in the glen.

'What was that?' Gail asked the question as they all stopped.

'Meredith's gone down to destroy a nest,' said An-

47

drew unconcernedly.

'A nest?'

'Of hooded crows. They build down there and it's a good opportunity to get rid of them. We don't allow the creatures to propagate their race if we can possibly avoid it.'

'I wish I could see Meredith,' said Robbie excitedly. 'Will he have taken all the eggs?'

'They'd hatched, Robbie. He's killed one of the parents, I expect, so he'll be dealing with the young——'

'But it's cruel—killing the babies, I mean,' gasped Gail, seeing, in her imagination, Meredith wringing their necks without the slightest compunction.

'You'd feel differently if you saw a sick and exhausted ewe with sightless holes where its eyes once had been.' He turned to her and smiled in an understanding sort of way. 'Life is tough and hard in the Highlands, Gail, and to you we might seem cruel, but you'll soon come to realize that we never kill for killing's sake. No stalker worth his salt would allow a nest of hooded crows to survive once he had found it.'

She said nothing and they walked some distance in silence. But after a while she murmured, almost to herself,

'All this is yours——' She made a comprehensive gesture with her hand. 'I haven't explored one hundredth part of it yet.'

'You've plenty of time.' He spoke in his customary clipped accents, but today there was a certain relaxing of his harsh and cold exterior. For the first time the shield was lowered and Gail sensed the heart beating under the armour still retained.

They reached the bank of the loch; away on the left a small building stood by the water's edge and Gail asked what it was.

'A fishing lodge.'

'You fish in the loch?' and when he nodded, 'You catch salmon?'

48

'The salmon are in the river,' Robbie instantly informed her.

'They jump up,' put in Shena. 'You should just see them jump!'

'Are they in our—in your river?' Gail wanted to know, looking up at her husband.

'They're in our river,' he replied, turning to her and stressing the word 'our'. 'But the fishing rights for salmon belong to the Duke.'

'That's all his land—on the other side of the river?'

'The river's the boundary, yes.'

'Would he know if you took the salmon from the stream?'

Andrew lifted his brows at that.

'Probably not—but we aren't in the habit of poaching.'

She flushed, but his mood led her to say,

'Not nowadays, but the Scots have a dreadful reputation.'

He laughed and Gail caught her breath. Louise had declared him to be the handsomest man she had ever seen, Gail suddenly recalled. . . .

'There was a time in our history when we did exist in a state of tribal warfare, preferring to rob our neighbours—or, even better, the wealthy effete English across the border.'

Gail laughed then.

'That's not very nice!'

'We *are* speaking of long, long ago,' he reminded her.

'Were you as bad as the historians make out?'

'I'm afraid so,' he admitted. 'You see, Scotland grew under the clan system; we had chieftains who themselves were barbaric even though they were also honourable and brave, descended as they were from the highest nobility in the land. Feuds brought out the worst in all participants and the bloodthirsty deeds committed have not been exaggerated.' He went on to expand and Gail listened with keen interest. How

49

different he was today, she thought, optimism welling up inside her. If they could remain friendly like this, could chat together and walk out with the children ... this was all she would ever ask; it was all she needed to make her feel secure, and that she really was a wife. For up till now she had been little more than a servant, a nanny to the children even though they addressed her as Mummy.

'Can we go along the burn?' Shena looked expectantly at her father. 'I don't want to go home yet.'

The sun was beginning to slant across the wild and lonely mountains, and the moorlands were taking on a rosy hue.

'We can't stay out much longer,' said Andrew. 'It gets chilly when the sun goes down.' A moment's hesitation and then, 'Very well, we have time to walk a little way along the burn.'

The clouds were fast becoming low and the view would soon be misted, but at present the sun was throwing everything into sharp relief and they stopped on a rise looking westwards to the magnificent view of Loch Tummel, and the wooded defile of the glen. To the north-east rose Ben-y-Gloe, with behind it several snow-capped peaks, scarred and fretted by ice action a very long while ago. Across the heather moors the herd of deer could still be seen, beginning to merge now with the landscape as the movement of the sun threw the hills behind them into shadow. Far down below the grey-roofed houses of the tiny village nestled in a hollow, scarcely noticeable, so well did they fit into the rural scene.

'Are the people all your tenants?' asked Gail after remarking on this attractive unity of buildings and landscape.

He shook his head.

'Most of the houses are owner-occupied, although a few are mine.'

'Owner-occupied?' She looked puzzled. 'But they're all exactly alike. Don't the owners want to alter them, or paint them different colours?' She herself would want a little individuality, she thought, if she owned one of the houses down there.

'They're not allowed to.'

'Not allowed? But you just said they were owner-occupied.'

'So they are.' He looked down at her and laughed. 'I expect that's another thing you will not agree with. All the tenants are subject to the Feu Charter; an agreement is drawn up when the house is sold and I make certain stipulations which must be observed. I would never allow any external alterations that would detract from the beauty of the village.'

'You mean,' she said in disbelief, 'that a feudal system still exists here?'

'Not in any way resembling the old feudal system,' he told her, clearly amused by her expression. 'But a landowner does still have certain rights which he maintains.' He glanced down at the village. 'You've just remarked on how well the village fits into the landscape. Would you have some of the houses painted white, or the roofs red or green?'

She shook her head emphatically.

'I see what you mean. No, I wouldn't, not now I come to think about it.'

'Well then. . . .' Andrew merely shrugged and left the rest unsaid, turning to seek the children who were chasing about among the trees above the glen.

Having a fair knowledge of the old feudal system Gail laughingly asked if the tenants still paid feudal dues and to her utter amazement he said yes, they did pay him feudal dues.

'I don't extort money from them,' he assured her. 'Each one pays something like ten shillings or a pound a year—I really wouldn't know. Sinclair looks to such things.'

'Sinclair works very hard.'

'He's an excellent man. I don't know what I'd do without him.'

The little burn frothed and spumed over the falls and rapids, its banks tree-clad and springy underfoot.

'We make our own electricity with it, don't we, Daddy?' Andrew smiled down at his son and nodded. 'The water goes through a pipe——' Robbie grabbed hold of Gail's hand. 'Come on and I'll show you. You see this pipe going down under the ground?—well, that leads to our hydro-electric station. Daddy built it!' he ended proudly.

'You built it?'

'Not alone; I helped.' He spoke casually as if such work was not in any way out of the ordinary for a man in his position. And as they turned homewards again after walking along the burn for a while, Gail fell to musing on his life, and on the kind of man he was. Married young to a beautiful woman—whose portrait still hung in the gallery; a child seven months later. And then the growing knowledge of his wife's infidelity. His forgiveness when he took her back ... twice he took her back, so he clearly considered the marriage tie as permanent—for better or worse. . . .

If he were a woman-hater it was natural—what with his wife's continued unfaithfulness and his daughter's careless flaunting of all the rules of chastity and honesty. But somehow Gail did not believe he was a woman-hater; she felt he would not be so unjust as to judge all women alike. Shame he had suffered, and disillusionment; those, and the humiliation caused by Morag's behaviour, must inevitably result in bitterness, and Gail felt that this in turn had brought about the harshness which was almost always apparent on the surface.

'Haven't we had a lovely time?' said Robbie enthusiastically as they neared the great grey house, bathed now in crimson and gold and orange as the sun sank lower in the sky. 'Will you come with us another day?'

'Yes, Robbie. I'll come with you next Sunday, if it's fine, of course.'

It had been a wonderful day altogether, mused Gail a long while later as, lying in her great white bed with its brass trimmings gleaming in the glow from her amber-shaded table-lamp, she went over it all again.

Church in the morning, and Robbie insisting on wearing his kilt 'just like Daddy'. Then lunch, with no Morag there to stir her father's wrath or send him into moody yet ominous silence. He had talked, and even allowed the children to chatter at the table, which was most unusual, as almost always he sternly ordered them to be quiet. And after that friendly, homely meal he had announced his intention of accompanying them on their customary Sunday afternoon stroll through part of the estate. Unable to conceal her pleasure, Gail had caught him looking oddly at her, examining her features in a new and searching way and automatically she had raised a hand to her temple.

For the first time she really did care about that scar.... Andrew never tolerated anything inferior, Morag had once said.

Afternoon tea had followed their walk; again Robbie and Shena were allowed to chatter, with their father sitting back in his chair, relaxed, and interestedly listening to them but glancing often at Gail and giving her a smile whenever she should meet his eyes.

If only it were always like this.... Yawning sleepily, she switched off the lamp and turned her head drowsily into the pillow.

But of course it was not always like that unforgettable Sunday. Morag returned on the Wednesday from her visit to friends and the more familiar strained atmosphere descended on Dunlochrie House. Even the servants were affected and instead of smiles dour faces were in evidence whenever one of them came into contact with the girl who seemed to cast a blight on everyone in the whole establishment.

On the Friday Gail returned from taking the children to school to find that Morag had risen earlier than usual. It was pouring with rain and a grey mist blotted out almost the entire view. Morag was sitting in a chair in the small room which was referred to as the snug. She had a glass in her hand and a cigarette dangling from her mouth.

'What weather! I'd go abroad if only I had some money!'

Gail stood looking down at her, wondering how anyone could drink whisky at this time of the day.

'Whom would you go with?' she inquired, unwilling to snub the girl by walking out the moment she had entered the room.

'You'd like to know, wouldn't you, Mrs. MacNeill?'

'I'm not particularly curious, Morag. I was merely making conversation.'

'You bore me with your goody-goody attitude. I don't expect, if the truth were known, that you're any better than the rest of us!'

'I never consider myself better than other people,' returned Gail gently. 'But I do have standards, and I adhere to them.'

Morag uttered an oath, then laughed as Gail shuddered.

'So pious!' Morag drew on her cigarette and inhaled deeply. 'I don't believe it's any more than a cover.' She leant forward in her chair, regarding Gail through narrowed eyes. 'If a wife doesn't get what she wants from her husband,' she said with slow deliberation, 'she begins to look elsewhere.'

'You appear very interested in my private life, Morag. I wonder why?'

The girl looked swiftly at her, then brought her lashes down, masking her expression.

'You'll not deceive my father, I warn you of that,' she said cryptically after a while.

'Would you mind being a little more explicit?'

'He has a very suspicious mind where women are concerned—so beware. Find yourself another man and he'll know immediately—unless you're very prudent, of course. My mother wasn't prudent—stupid woman. I'd be much more careful with my husband.'

Gail went white; she felt physically sick, and yet at the same time sorry for this girl. Was it really her fault that she was so objectionable?—or was it merely a matter of genetics?

'Do you think you'll find a husband, carrying on the way you do?'

'I could marry now were I old enough.' She shrugged her shoulders and, draining her glass, refilled it from the bottle on the table at her side. 'I'm not so sure I want to get married; there's much more fun to be had without it.'

To what depths would she ultimately sink? Gail wondered. To what further shame and disgrace was Andrew to be subjected? Must he carry the cross to his dying day? Gail shivered at the thought—and tried again.

'Morag, why can't we be friends? If you want to go abroad I'll ask your father if we can all go—when Robbie and Shena are on holiday from school. Would you like that?'

'Go away with anyone like you?' A derisive laugh rang out. 'Have to listen to your sanctimonious preachings, and be hampered by those insufferable brats! Not likely. I'm going on my own—at least, with a friend of my own choosing,' she amended.

Gail said more curtly,

'Your father won't give you money for that.'

'He might be glad to, when I've finished with him!'

'You ought to be locked in your room!'

'He's tried that. For four whole days! I wrecked the place. It cost him a small fortune to put it right.' Again her glass was emptied, and again Morag refilled it. 'He has more sense than to make the same mistake again.'

'Do you really believe you can continue defying him like this?'

'What can he do about it?'

'He could cast you off, completely. Have you never

55

thought of that?'

'He never cast my mother off——'

'We'll not bring your mother into it, Morag,' interrupted Gail sharply, and another grating laugh rang out.

'Naturally you won't want to talk about her. She's a shadow blotting out any future for you. Father adored her and her memory will always be with him.' She paused, watching Gail's expression. 'I suppose someone has told you about her?'

'I'm not discussing your mother, Morag.' Gail moved towards the door and opened it.

'Someone *has* told you about her, it's plain to see,' jeered Morag, but Gail did not turn her head. 'He took her back twice—twice! Doesn't that prove he adored her? She was beautiful—and flawless!'

Gail whipped round.

'What do you mean by that?'

'Just what I say.' Morag looked rather blank and Gail sagged with relief. 'My mother was beautiful, and perfect. Father loved her because of that. I told·you he tolerates nothing inferior.' Morag was going on to talk about her mother's portrait, but Gail walked out, her head erect, but a quivering sigh on her lips as she made her way up to the quiet privacy of her room.

The dead Mrs. MacNeill was a shadow blotting out any future for Gail. Andrew loved her ... had taken her back twice.... She had been flawless....

What did it matter? Gail occupied the position she had expected to occupy on accepting Andrew's proposal of marriage. She mothered the children, contributed to the running of·the house. On the evenings when Andrew had guests he had treated her as a husband should, subjecting her to no trace of embarrassment or humiliation. His friendly attitude was for the sake of appearances, certainly, but she expected nothing else.

No, the ever-present memory of his dead wife could in no way affect Gail's life ... and yet why was she weighed down by a strange heaviness all at once? Somewhere, away in her subconscious, dwelt the sort of void experienced when one reaches out, groping and floundering, searching for some elusive, nebulous thing.

CHAPTER FOUR

ANOTHER quarrel was taking place, but this time Gail prudently kept out of it. However, she soon learned what it was about, for Morag came up to the nursery where Gail was going through the children's clothes, seeing what she could send to the local jumble sale.

'All his money, and he won't give me a couple of hundred pounds!' Morag's face was red, her eyes blazing with fury. 'The mean, parsimonious creature. I hate him!'

Gail was examining a dress of Shena's; it was almost new and she hesitated. But it would not fit Shena by the time the weather was warm enough to wear it, Gail decided, putting it on top of the pile of clothes already on the chair.

'Perhaps,' she said, turning to the drawer again, 'you would have a better chance of success if you went about it a little differently.'

'Yes?' Morag's fair brows lifted. 'You never appear to be short. Give me some advice.'

'I'm not in the mood to be played with. If you've nothing interesting to say then please leave me to get on with my task.' Gail was bending over the drawer; when she straightened up Morag was standing very close, an almost savage expression on her face.

'Who do you think you are?—speaking to me like this? Me, Morag MacNeill!'

'No doubt you are somebody,' Gail frankly owned, but added, 'Unfortunately for you I judge people not on their status in the hierarchy of our society but on the way they conduct themselves. You go out of your way to be disagreeable to everyone in general and to me in particular. I've tried to be friends—I wanted to be friends with you, but you're determined to throw my offers of friendship back at me and, frankly, I've come to the end of my patience.'

'I could slap your face!'

'I don't advise it, Morag.' She held up a blouse and assessed the size. 'I requested you to leave me.'

'I'll leave when it pleases me. This is my father's house and you're nothing more than an interloper—a glorified servant!' Taking a packet of cigarettes from her pocket, Morag lit one, deliberately blowing the smoke in Gail's face and laughing as she stepped back. 'About this money—I asked you for advice.' Gail ignored her and she snapped harshly, 'Answer me! How do you get round him? He showers money on you, but I have nothing!'

'I receive an allowance, as I expect you do. We choose to spend it differently, that's all.' Her nerves were quivering; these arguments with Morag always left her weak, and strangely bereft of hope. Why the future prospect should be dimmed by this girl Gail did not know. She would always be there, to make life uncomfortable, but Gail had accepted that from first admitting defeat. Nowadays she felt drained after a clash with Morag, as if fearing the girl would put a permanent blight on her life.

'I'd like to know how much you get,' Morag was saying. 'Are you feathering your nest in case he throws you out when Robbie and Shena no longer need you?'

When they no longer needed her. . . ? Gail had never thought of that. But had not Andrew stressed the fact of the permanence of the marriage? The arrangement would be binding, he said, very binding. He would never send her away after saying a thing like that.

'Are you feathering your nest?' repeated Morag when Gail did not speak.

'I save because I'm naturally thrifty.' Closing the drawer, Gail picked up the pile of clothes from the chair and left the room, fully aware of the scowling gaze that followed her.

She dropped the clothes off on her way to pick up Shena and Robbie.

59

'Thank you very much. These are lovely.' Mrs. Stuart was in charge of the sale, which was to be held in aid of charity. 'I suppose you're off to pick up the wee ones—or have you time for a cup of tea?'

'It's kind of you to ask,' smiled Gail, wishing she had come out a few minutes earlier so that she could have accepted. 'But I shall be only just in time. I've some toys to sort out and I'll stay and have a cup of tea with you when I bring those.'

'Thank you, Mrs. MacNeill. I shall look forward to that.'

Morag was nowhere to be seen when Gail returned home with the children, and over an hour later, on hearing a car drive on to the forecourt Gail went to the window and saw Morag getting out of the runabout. Gail had known she could drive, often having seen her on the estate, but to take a car on the public road. . . . True, she looked at least eighteen, but the police hereabouts must know her. Gail actually experienced a fleeting moment of fear lest Morag had been pulled up, but the girl was nonchalantly taking a cardboard box and two parcels from the back of the car. Gail frowned. How could she have been shopping if she had no money?

Light, running footsteps were heard on the stairs, and the slamming of Morag's bedroom door. Purposefully Gail followed, entering the room without ceremony. Morag, holding a dress against her, twisted and turned before the mirror.

'What do you want?' she demanded, staring at Gail through the mirror. 'How dare you come into my room without being invited?'

'What do you mean by taking a car on the road?' snapped Gail, coming further into the room.

Slowly and disbelievingly Morag turned. Never before had Gail questioned her like this, or interfered in any way at all with her actions.

'And what is that to do with you? When I'm away I drive my friends' cars all the time. Get out, and look to the children. That's what you're here for!'

She drove her friends' cars.... They, it would appear, were as stupid as Morag.

'Did you not consider the consequences of discovery? The police round here must know you're under age.'

Morag's teeth snapped together.

'Go away, for pity's sake! You bore me to distraction with your law-abiding piety. Why should you care about the consequences? You've no concern for me.'

'My concern at present happens to be for your father.'

'It does?' Morag's eyes opened wide. 'How very interesting. Have you fallen for him by any chance? Women do——' She threw back her head and laughed. 'But how priceless! Unrequited love! Wait till I tell the crowd—oh, this will provide some laughs for us!'

Gail went white, but this time it was with temper. Only now did she fully appreciate her husband's feelings when he had struck the girl.

'Are you quite shameless! Don't you care anything about your father's humiliation when you're prosecuted?—which you are bound to be some time if, as you say, you're driving cars without a licence.'

'Stop preaching!' Morag's face was crimson with anger and hate. 'Get out of my room!'

Gail went, there being nothing else she could do, but she meant to inform Andrew of what had occurred. She would have an opportunity this evening, when they were alone after dinner. Tale-carrying was loathsome to her, but Andrew must be warned.

Morag was never late for dinner; this was one thing in which she was forced to obey her father. Were she only a minute late he would order her place to be cleared and should she desire to eat she did so in another room.

Her place was cleared that evening, and for some reason Gail was uneasy.

'Is Morag in?' she blurted out at last.

61

'In? I expect so. What makes you ask?' Andrew glanced across at Gail, frowning at her expression.

'I'm not sure why I asked, but—but I feel she might have gone out.' She put down her knife and fork with a nervous movement. Was Morag out in the car again?— and in the dark? Suppose she knocked someone down...? 'Andrew ... she took the car out this afternoon, to do her shopping——'

'Took the car?' he interrupted sharply. 'Are you sure?'

'I didn't like to interfere, because I know her actions have nothing to do with me, but I saw her drive on to the forecourt and tackled her about taking the car on to the public road.'

An awful silence fell on the room; Andrew's face was like thunder. Morag had not been pulled up, Gail hastened to tell him, but his features retained their lines of dark fury. He rose from his chair and left the room. Gail bit her lip, feeling guilty and wondering if there was a better way in which she could have handled the situation. If only Morag would listen to reason; if only she were not so defiant, and determinedly aggressive.

When Andrew returned his anger had subsided somewhat, but his face was harsh and his eyes were dark and brooding.

'She's gone to stay with friends,' he informed Gail. 'She left a note on the hall table. She got one of the men to drive her to the station.'

'So she hasn't taken the car?' Gail breathed a sigh of relief, but she was puzzled too and she added, 'She didn't say anything to me about visiting friends.'

'She's gone for a fortnight—so she says in her note.' This was the first time Andrew had discussed Morag with her since the day he admitted she was lost to him. He sat down but made no attempt to touch his food. 'You say she went shopping? What did she buy?'

'A dress, but I don't know what else.'

'She told me she had no money.' He became thoughtfully silent for a space and then, 'You didn't lend her any?' he asked in threatening tones, and Gail shook her head. But she felt a prickling sensation in the region of her spine. Why should she be recalling Morag's insolent questions regarding her allowance...? 'I save,' Gail had said.

Her money was kept in a small trinket box on the dressing-table; it was unlocked because Gail had never yet had an experience which led to distrust. She had lived with her parents, and then her sister, and here at Dunlochrie House she knew the servants were trustworthy, otherwise they would not be employed by Andrew. As soon as dinner was over she ran upstairs and opened the box. Empty. Over a hundred pounds had been in the box—the whole of this month's allowance, given her by Andrew, and savings from her previous allowances.

'What weather! I'd go abroad if only I had some money.' Morag's words hammered at Gail's brain. Had Morag gone abroad ... with a boy-friend, as she had done once before, unashamedly stealing money for that purpose? What should she do? Trembling, Gail stood there, staring at the empty box, confused and uncertain, and blaming herself for leaving her money about —putting temptation in Morag's way.

But she did not remain undecided for long. If Morag had gone abroad nothing could be done about it at this stage, for both her present whereabouts and her destination were unknown. And there was nothing to be gained by informing Andrew of the theft and subjecting him to further humiliation—a humiliation that would be far greater than any before, Morag having robbed his wife. No, saving her husband's pride was far more important than the loss of her money.

As was to be expected the rest of the evening was ruined, dragging slowly through the brooding silence into which Andrew had fallen. Twice Gail tried to open up a conversation; she was answered in monosyllables harshly and impatiently uttered. Yet as the days passed the customary lightness enveloped the whole household; everyone, including Andrew, seemed to be different with Morag out of the way and Gail could have wished her grown up and married were she not heartily sorry for the man who would eventually become Morag's husband.

On the Wednesday the children were off school, it being a holiday, but as they both had slight colds Gail did not take them out, for although the weather was dry, the air was crisp and chill, with a mist topping the mountains and the ground underfoot damp after the recent rains.

Mrs. Davis called just after lunch; having heard of the holiday she wished to take Robbie and Shena to her home. She would bring them back after tea, she said.

'I didn't want them to go out,' Gail began, wondering how high her authority stood on an occasion like this. 'They both have colds and I'm keeping them warm.' She and the children were sitting cosily by the fire, playing a card game, and there was no mistaking the disappointment on their faces at the suggestion of their going out with their grandmother.

Mrs. Davis stared arrogantly down at her, still in her outdoor things, having refused Gail's offer of taking her coat.

'They'll be quite all right in the car,' she snapped. 'Come, Robbie and Shena, go and fetch your coats.'

Gail bit her lip; both children were looking questioningly at her, their mouths drooping.

'It's very cold, Mrs. Davis——'

'I'm taking my daughter's children out! Kindly get them ready!'

'I don't want to go,' said Robbie with unaccustomed crossness. 'We're playing games with Mummy.'

'I don't want to go either.' Shena sat back more comfortably in her chair, examining the cards in her hand.

The older woman's face reddened.

'Such ill manners! I must see Andrew about this.

64

Obviously you're not doing what you're paid to do!'

'Paid, Mrs. Davis?' Gail's brows lifted in a gesture of arrogance equal to that of the woman standing above her. 'That's an odd expression to use to a wife.'

Black fury settled on Mrs. Davis's thin and painted face.

'It will not pay you to be insolent with me,' she snapped. 'You might be Andrew's wife, but as he married you for the specific purpose of looking after my daughter's children, you're no more than a paid servant.' Gail said nothing; her anger died, destroyed by the hurtful knowledge that what this woman said was true. She and Morag had been discussing her, that was for sure, Mrs. Davis's words being similar to those already used by her granddaughter on more than one occasion. 'Kindly get them ready,' the woman ordered, but turned to Shena. 'Do as you're told and get your coat. Robbie, you too! You're both coming out with me.'

Shena started to cry, and began to cough. If only Andrew were about, thought Gail distractedly, then his would be the decision. But he was away across the fields, clad in overalls, assisting his joiner with the posts required for the fencing off of a new plantation of fir trees. They had grown to the stage when the roe deer would eat them, and fencing was very necessary both for the protection of the saplings and of the deer, for were they to get into the plantation the deer would have to be shot, and most farmers were loath to kill these dainty Bambi-like creatures unnecessarily.

As she sat there in a state of uncertainty Gail uttered a little sigh. This was one of those occasions when it was starkly brought home to her that she was indeed neither wife nor mother. Had she been a wife her husband's support for all her actions would have been assured; were she a mother her authority regarding the children would have been paramount.

'If you must take them then I really can't prevent you,' she admitted reluctantly, avoiding Robbie's eyes.

'But please keep them warm. Andrew wouldn't be very pleased were they to be ill.'

A short while later they were in the car, Robbie sulky and silent and Shena still showing evidence of her recent tears. Gail stood watching the car disappearing down the drive, waving to Robbie who was kneeling on the back seat, staring out of the window.

Andrew came back at tea time, driving the Land-Rover. He inquired after the children and Gail told him where they had gone, adding rather haltingly,

'It was cold, and I didn't want them to go out——'

'Their grandmother naturally wants to see them,' he interrupted before she could mention their colds. 'She has my permission to take them out on occasions. It's some time since their grandfather saw them; he's bedridden—I don't think I've mentioned that. He's a lonely man, and loves Robbie and Shena. It does him good to see them.'

Gail felt better after that. It was only right for the children to visit their grandfather. She fell to thinking about this unknown man whom Andrew said was lonely. How did he fare with a wife like Mrs. Davis? Gail had always imagined her to be a widow, as her husband had never been mentioned either by Andrew or any of the three children.

Immediately they returned Gail saw that Shena was ill. Her big blue eyes were bright and watering, her cheeks flushed and her nose running. Gail took out a handkerchief and wiped it, at the same time feeling the child's forehead. It was burning.

'You're right about their colds,' said Mrs. Davis, but lacking any graciousness of manner. 'Shena is making much more of hers than is necessary, but then she's become even more spoiled than ever lately. Put her to bed, she'll be all right in the morning. There's no need to call the doctor.'

But both Andrew and Gail thought otherwise, and it was soon established that Shena had influenza, and a severe chill on her stomach as well.

66

'She must have been ill before she went out.' Andrew stood on one side of the child's bed and Gail on the other, the doctor having only just left.'

'I knew she had a cold——'

'Then you should have kept her in,' he snapped in angry surprise. 'Would you have sent her to school?'

'I don't think so—but I didn't have to make the decision,' she hurriedly pointed out, 'because they had this holiday. Her cold was not really noticeable until after lunch——'

'And yet you let her go out?' The sharp keen edge to his tone left her speechless for a moment. Had he forgotten voicing his approval of their going out with their grandmother?

'I did say,' she managed at last, 'that I didn't want them to go with Mrs. Davis, but you said it was all right.'

'You didn't tell me Shena was ill—in any case, you'd already let them go.' Shena gave a little moan and he bent down, over the bed, placing a cool hand on her damp forehead. 'I absolutely fail to understand how you could have been so unobservant as not to realize just how ill she was. She should have been in bed hours ago!'

The blame and censure in his voice and the injustice of his words brought the quick tears pressing against the back of Gail's eyes. Her life was difficult enough without her husband adding his contribution.

'I was keeping them warm,' she was forced to say in her own defence. 'They were by the fire all day until Mrs. Davis came and said she wanted to take them to her home for tea. Had she not taken them I'm sure I'd have put Shena to bed quite early in the afternoon.' Shena was whimpering and as Andrew had moved away Gail sat down on the bed, replacing the covers which the restless child was in the process of throwing off.

'Why didn't you tell Mrs. Davis that Shena had a cold?' His blue eyes fixed her angrily. 'I can't understand your carelessness!'

'I'm afraid,' returned Gail with sudden indignation, 'that Mrs. Davis was insistent.'

'She couldn't have insisted had you raised a strong enough objection——' Gail made to interrupt, but an imperious wave of his hand cut her short even before the first word was out. 'The children are in your charge and I expect you to use your judgement where their welfare is concerned.'

Gail was tempted to ascertain here and now just how far her authority went, but Shena was tossing and turning and still fretfully whimpering. It was not the time for questions of that nature; besides, Andrew was not in the right mood, his gaze being one of angry accusation not unmingled with puzzlement, and it struck Gail that he might almost be thinking she had wanted to be rid of the children, for an hour or two. He should have known better than that, though. Surely he could see she was happiest when Robbie and Shena were with her.

For several days Shena was very poorly, but care and warmth and the love Gail bestowed on her at last had their effect and not only did the child begin to improve physically, but she also drew very close to Gail during the second half of the period she remained in bed. This was just over a week and on the day she was to get up Andrew was there to carry her down to the snug where a huge log fire burned despite the adequacy of the central heating.

'There, how's that?' Gently he laid her down on the couch, against the pillows Gail had placed there. 'Warm?'

'Lovely and warm, Daddy, thank you.' Her smile, though, was for both of them as her beautiful eyes moved from him to Gail. No reserve now or cautious withdrawal; Shena had been completely won over during her illness and Gail sent up a little prayer of thankfulness as she sat with her, telling her stories and bringing her drinks and finally easing her down and

68

drawing the curtains together when at last Shena wanted to go to sleep.

Andrew went for Robbie, whose cold had kept him off school only a couple of days, a circumstance that gave him scant satisfaction. Aware of all the attention being lavished on his sister, he was clearly disgusted at his own healthy resistance and considered himself in some way cheated.

'I'm not well at all,' he had declared when Gail pronounced him fit for school. 'It's my tummy. I think I've got gout. My great-grandfather had gout.'

'You usually have gout in your feet,' laughed Gail, fixing his scarf and buttoning his coat up to it. 'Never in your stomach, Robbie, so you'll have to think of something else.'

He had thought of something else—several things in fact, but as the mention of these merely brought laughter to Gail's or Andrew's lips Robbie finally took umbrage and gave up the fight. But he did warn them darkly that should he die through their neglect they would be sorry for the rest of their lives.

During her tender care for Shena Andrew seemed to be seeing Gail for the first time as she really was, watching her at times with an altogether new expression that brought the colour to her cheeks, and a strange yearning to her heart. Involuntarily then she would put up a hand to feel the scar through her hair and wish that she had gone into hospital when her doctor suggested it, and had the scar removed. It was not too late, of course, but Gail could not now leave the children. Besides, she did not want her husband to know the scar had ever been there. The reason for this eluded her ... or perhaps it was that she did not desire too close a probe into her feelings....

Robbie came bounding into the snug and Gail instantly put a finger to her lips.

'Hush,' she whispered. 'Shena's asleep.'

'She's up, though.' Robbie came close and whispered in her ear. 'Is she going to school tomorrow?'

69

Gail shook her head, smiling in amusement and glancing towards the door as Andrew entered the darkened room.

'Not for at least a week.'

Robbie pouted.

'It's not fair! She must be better if she's up.'

'I'm not really up,' protested Shena, awakened by the whispering and movements in the room. 'I'm only half up, aren't I, Mummy?'

'Yes, darling, you're only half up.'

'How's my baby?' Andrew came close, his face tanned and glowing with health from the outdoor life he led; his mouth was softened by the flickering firelight, his thick dark hair a little tousled by the frolics of the west wind, howling now around the house and swaying the graceful conifers as it swept away over the wild and heathered grouse moors. He bent over his young daughter; she sat up and flung her arms around his neck. He received a loud kiss on the cheek. 'I'm not a baby,' she said then, and her father promptly retorted,

'In that case you won't want to be nursed.'

'Were you going to nurse me?' she asked, her face falling.

'I was indeed—right here on my knee.' He sat down by the fire, his eyes still on her. 'Whom shall I nurse instead—Robbie?'

'No—nurse Mummy!' It was Robbie who spoke. A man like me being nursed! his indignant glance seemed to be saying.

Silence followed his words. Andrew's eyes on her, half-searching, half-amused, brought the blood rushing to Gail's face. She did not know how adorable she looked in the firelight glow, that her delicate features were enchantingly brought into relief, even though shadowed faintly by the long sweep of silken lashes lowered to hide the dreamy, half-yearning expression in her beautiful brown eyes.

'Mummies don't be nursed,' said Shena on a scoffing note. 'They're too big!'

70

'Our mummy isn't too big—because she's a lot smaller than Daddy. She only comes up to his shoulders!'

Discomfort overwhelming her, Gail rose hastily and drew back the curtains, letting in the light. Andrew's eyes were still upon her as she came back to her chair—on her face and then her neck and fleetingly on the slender curves of her body.

'Are you going to let Daddy nurse you?' she asked Shena, a sudden vision of her scarred body coming into her mind. Stooping, she picked up the soft lambswool dressing-gown and held it open, her glance questioning, and encouraging.

'Yes ... but I'm not a baby. Big girls are nursed sometimes, aren't they?'

'Big girls of five and a half, yes, of course they are,' said Andrew, giving his attention at last to his small and lovely daughter.

She sat on his knee, swinging her legs, one arm around his neck. Robbie stood there, glancing at her now and then from under his small brows, his mouth tight and his fingers tapping the arm of Gail's chair. Understandingly she put an arm around his waist, drawing him close to her. This much he did not mind, obviously, because his face brightened and his dark curly head rested against Gail's breast. Andrew had noticed Gail's action and although his eyes were soft and his mouth relaxed a frown settled on his brow. Gail looked at him, feeling he was recalling his anger at her allowing Shena to go out when she had a cold, and that he was actually chiding himself for being unjust. His anger had not only lasted, she recalled with a little pang, it had increased as the days went by and Shena's condition worsened. But as she improved so his anger died and his way with Gail became less rigid and accusing. She had not yet asked him how far her authority went, and as time passed she found greater difficulty in broaching the subject. Phrasing was not easy with such a delicate subject, for the last impres-

71

sion Gail wanted to give was that of possessiveness. The children were not hers; Gail accepted this just as she accepted the right of their grandmother to see them as often as she wished, and to ask Andrew if it were her right to withhold her permission for this seemed all wrong. Some day, she thought, a suitable occasion might arise when the subject could be broached; until then she could only hope she would not be faced with such a problem again.

Robbie stirred against her and she smiled at him. Shena's dark head was resting comfortably under her father's chin and Robbie snuggled closer. It was an intimate, homely scene ... with only one link of love missing, mused Gail in an abstracted way. She and Andrew loved the children; the children loved them, and they also loved one another....

'Do you want tea now?' she asked Andrew. He was not often with them at this time of day, but since Shena's illness he had been taking Robbie to school in the morning and bringing them home in the afternoon. So he took tea with them, it having been laid in Shena's room until today.

'When you're ready,' returned Andrew obligingly. 'I'm not particularly hungry, but I expect Robbie is.' He leant away from Shena. 'What about you?'

'I'm hungry. I want sandwiches and scones and jam and biscuits.'

'Then I'd better see to it. We can't have our invalid feeling hungry.'

'Will Morag be sorry I've been poorly?' asked Shena as they were having tea half an hour later, and it struck Gail, as it had on so many occasions, how distant the older girl was from the other two. She rarely mentioned them and they rarely mentioned her. Morag never took them out, never bought them a book or other present. She could have derived such pleasure from them, and they from her—had she not been so utterly lacking in patience and understanding.

'I don't expect so,' replied Andrew, his eyes suddenly

glinting at the mention of the girl. So peaceful it had been, these past days since Morag's departure, and to Gail's knowledge Andrew had never so much as tried to discover where the girl was. Probably he knew from bitter experience that he would only be wasting his time. Morag came and went as she liked, accounting to no one, obeying no rules. Often Gail tried to think of an effective way of dealing with such a person, and soon realized that if an effective way had existed Andrew would never have accepted failure. Strong as he was, with that wild Highland temper, and lawlessness and murder in his blood, he could not control that wilful girl. In the past, yes—she would soon have been brought to heel, would no doubt have cried out for mercy before being ruthlessly dealt with, but these days violence was not permitted. And it seemed to Gail, distasteful though the idea might be, that violence was the only method of subduing a girl like Morag. What was to become of her? Would she marry, and make some poor man's life a misery?—or would she remain single, and give her father no peace for the rest of his days?

'Where is Morag, Daddy?' Robbie was stuffing too much in his mouth. The merest frown from his father caused him to put the rest of the sandwich down on his plate.

'Away on holiday.' His eyes flickered go Gail, and moved instantly away again. Gail changed the subject.

'What have you been doing at school today, Robbie?'

'Sums and writing, and drawing and nature. We were learning about foxes and I said they were taking our lambs and Miss Spencer let me tell the class all about it. I liked doing that; I'm going to be a schoolteacher when I grow up.'

'So you can tell the children about foxes, eh?' Andrew buttered a scone for Shena and put it on her plate. 'You want some jam, you said?' He held the pot in his hand and made to spoon some out.

'Yes, but I don't like that kind.'

'What kind do you like?'

'Red jam—that's black.'

'I keep trying to get her to eat blackcurrant,' Gail admitted ruefully. 'However, I'll fetch the strawberry.'

'Don't get up,' he said, frowning slightly. 'Ring the bell.' This thought for her was something entirely new, and Gail felt a tinge of pleasure at his unexpected consideration.

'Has Meredith shot the foxes?' Robbie asked as Gail rang the bell. Meredith was the estate stalker and he had been out several nights running making his rounds of the known dens. Last night Andrew had been out with him, and a stalker from another estate too. The den was in a cairn, and the cubs had been accounted for by the terriers. But the parents had been away and the three men posted themselves around the cairn, waiting for their return. Darkness fell, but the men remained close to the cairn, for sooner or later the dog and vixen must return. In the crannies round the den the men dozed, but were repeatedly jerked into wakefulness by the scalp-prickling cry of the vixen calling to her unresponding young. She had known humans were about and kept her distance, but with the first light of dawn her maternal instinct brought her to the cairn—to fall victim to an instant-killing shot from Andrew's gun. The dog had escaped, too wary to return to the den. His turn would come another time. The men had been out again today on another hunt. This time the vixen was in the cairn. She had been bolted by the terriers and shot, while again the plucky little dogs scoured the labyrinthine, airless darkness to dispatch the cubs. One of the terriers had been trapped, and the great stones of the cairn had had to be removed one by one in order to free him. He came out as cheerful and dauntless as ever, even though his coat was matted with peat and filth.

'Some of them, Robbie,' Andrew was saying. 'We shan't be losing so many lambs now.'

'Is it only in litter time that they attack the sheep?'

74

Gail wanted to know.

'Usually. A fox on its own can live on rabbits and voles during the summer, and of course there is carrion in winter.' Sick and aged deer provided this carrion, and other animals which also had succumbed to the harsh and merciless winter of the Highlands.

Gail had thought she would never get used to this killing, but she was surprised now at her own admission that it was necessary. Those cuddly little cubs were undoubtedly attractive, but unfortunately they grew up, and attacking a litter was the only way to keep the numbers down. One vixen, shot soon after Gail's arrival, was carrying no less than ten unborn cubs.

'You're getting used to our way of life,' Andrew commented as if reading her thoughts.

She nodded.

'Yes, I'm getting used to it.'

'Will you learn to shoot?' asked Robbie eagerly, and this time Gail shook her head vigorously.

'No, Robbie,' she replied with emphasis. 'I will not learn to shoot.'

CHAPTER FIVE

MORAG had not returned at the end of a fortnight, and Andrew's face was becoming anxious and drawn. Suspecting he had been making tentative inquiries Gail felt deeply for him, understanding that his position necessitated the avoidance of any move which might result in unsavoury publicity. His face also portrayed a tiredness due to his sitting or lying around in the cold and mist of a Highland gloaming, or the icy dampness of boggy earth at dawn. For the annual fox den attacking which always took place at cubbing time must be relentlessly continued if the inevitable lamb losses were to be kept down to a minimum.

As the days went by and Morag was still absent his mounting anxiety alternated with a moroseness manifested in an attitude of almost complete indifference to his wife. She might not be there at all, and Gail would often experience that strange little void within her, a void which was now more in the nature of a loss than the vague reaching out to grasp vainly at some unknown thing far beyond her reach.

On Shena's first morning back at school he came in as Gail and the two children were having their breakfast, his eyes rimmed with tiredness, his overalls caked with mud, and particles of damp earth adhering to his hair.

'Will you do me a favour?' he asked, looking down at her from his great height. She nodded and he went on. 'I have a list here of what Johnson needs for the fencing—bolts and screws and clips and things—and I wondered if, when you've dropped Shena and Robbie off at school, you'll go on to Perth and get them for me?'

'Yes, of course.'

He then went on to tell her where the shop was, adding,

'Use your own money and I'll settle up with you later. You have plenty?' and without giving her the chance to reply, 'Of course you have. I remember your saying you save most of your allowance. I'm going up now to get a bath and some sleep,' and before Gail could say what she wanted to say he had left the room.

Use your own money. . . .

She rose with the intention of going after him, seeking desperately for words to explain why she was short of money, but Shena chose that moment to poke a spoon into her glass of milk, with the result that the glass toppled over.

'Clumsy,' chuckled Robbie. 'Now your nice clean dress is all wet!'

Gail glanced at the closed door, then at the clock, and gave a deep sigh. There was nothing for it but to change Shena's dress right away, and as this made them late Gail decided to take the children to school and then come back for the money. But on arrival she discovered to her dismay that Andrew was already in bed.

'Didn't he have his breakfast?' she inquired of Mrs. Birchan, the housekeeper.

'Not a bite,' the woman replied disgustedly. 'A good bowl of porridge would have put some warmth into him after being out all night. But there you are—men are so stubborn you never can get anywhere with them!'

Listening by the dividing door a few minutes later Gail could not hear a sound, and on knocking on the outer door she received no response. Silently turning the handle, she opened the door and peeped into the room. The curtains were drawn together; Andrew was fast asleep in bed, his hair, newly-washed and still wet, appearing darker than ever against the snowy whiteness of the pillow. She bit her lip. To waken him was unthinkable, yet she must have the money to get the joiner's requirements. These were urgent because the roe deer had already found the plantation and shots were having to be fired into the air in order to scare them away.

Gail felt she could have choked Morag.

Andrew stirred in his sleep; reluctantly and dejectedly Gail went forward into the room and stood by the bed.

'Andrew,' she whispered. No response, and she repeated his name in her normal voice. On opening his eyes he frowned uncomprehendingly for a space and then jerked himself into a sitting position.

'What's wrong?' he demanded sharply and she knew his thoughts were on Morag.

'Nothing serious,' she hastened to assure him.

'Then what do you want?' Anger and impatience edged his voice, and although she was strangely hurt Gail could understand how he felt, being woken like this from his well-earned sleep.

'Those things you asked me to get—I haven't enough money. . . .' She tailed off at his look of surprise.

'They'll only come to about ten or twelve pounds.'

'I haven't that much.' What must he think? she wondered miserably, his having remarked less than an hour ago on her having told him she saved most of her allowance.

'I see.' His voice was clipped. He did not see at all, his glance clearly said. In fact she felt sure he did not believe her and she added swiftly,

'I wouldn't have wakened you, Andrew, had I the money.'

'Very well.' He waved her out of the room as he spoke. 'I'll get it from the safe.'

Anger and unhappiness possessed her as she drove down to Perth. If Andrew didn't believe her then he must be thinking she had refused to lend him the money in case it was not refunded; if he did believe her then he must be wondering how she had spent it as,

78

apart from picking up the children, she scarcely ever went out.

A rift resulted from the incident; Andrew's coolness and indifference increased, and often intruding into Gail's mind was her sister's firm assertion that he did not like women.

She felt she hated Morag, and indeed when she did eventually arrive home, her new deep tan telling its own story, Gail instantly tackled her and, the fleeting blush being all she needed, she tore into the girl, revealing her temper for the first time since coming to Dunlochrie. Taken by surprise, Morag was speechless for a while, but on making a recovery she flatly denied having stolen the money.

'I don't believe you! Nothing you can say will convince me you didn't take the money! Where have you been all this time, anyway?'

'To the sun! Are you jealous?'

Gail raked her with disdain.

'Your father's been out of his mind with worry——'

'Rubbish! He doesn't care where I go or what I do. He's glad to get me out of the house.'

'One could scarcely blame him for that, if it were true. But it isn't true. You're only fifteen and still under his care and authority. If you had any feelings for him you'd try to behave.'

'Well, I haven't any feelings for him, never have had. I've no feelings for anyone. It's better that way because you can't ever get hurt. Mother never had any feelings for anyone, and so her life was happy.'

'There's no happiness without love, Morag,' said Gail, more quietly now. 'For your father's sake, why don't you try?'

Morag sighed exasperatedly.

'Your preachings! Don't you ever stop to think what a ridiculous figure you make, standing there, with that pious air of superiority? Why don't you give up? You're not here to convert me, but to make sure those two sweet little idols don't follow my degenerate and

79

downhill path.' She laughed and actually made to flick Gail's cheek with her finger, but Gail stepped back, utter dislike in her eyes. 'Have you told Father I took the money?' asked Morag curiously after a pause.

'Your father has quite enough to worry him!'

'Oh, yes. . . . Your concern,' mocked Morag, staring at Gail with assumed pity. 'The wife, shielding her poor harassed husband from knowledge of his daughter's wanton ways.' She cocked a commiserating glance at Gail. 'And he doesn't even notice his lovelorn wife—or has there been a change since I went away?'

A change for the worse, brought on by your dishonesty, Gail could have said, but pride prevented her.

'I shall expect the return of every penny you stole,' she began, but was cut short with a derisive laugh.

'Some hope! I've said I didn't take it—and I stick to that. One of the servants must have robbed you—if you've been robbed!'

'You're utterly shameless!'

Unconcernedly taking a packet of cigarettes from her handbag, Morag flipped it open.

'That's what Father says, so you obviously agree on one thing.' Lighting a cigarette, Morag blew the smoke across the room towards Gail, as she had done once before.

Almost suffocated with disgust, Gail turned to the door.

'You're a disgrace to your sex!' she exclaimed, and left her.

Another quarrel took place between father and daughter on Andrew's return to the house at teatime. Although present when it began—Andrew being either forgetful of her presence or deliberately ignoring it—Gail soon made her departure. But whatever had happened this time Morag was surprisingly reduced to tears. However, the conflict was also taking its toll where Andrew himself was concerned. His harshness was terrible to see—and invariably it was Gail who came in for the brunt of it.

She seemed to be blamed for everything that went wrong; if one of the children happened to be naughty she was icily censured, as she also was when, on taking in a parcel from the postman one day, she forgot to give it to her husband immediately he came in. He snapped at her for running out of petrol on her way to bring the children from school one day, and again when she allowed them to stay up a little later than usual.

Gail bore it all patiently, excusing his conduct because of the trouble Morag was giving him. Nevertheless, she was only human and resentment began to mount. This was to reach a climax one day when, she and Andrew having been invited to a ball at the Castle, he said, with what she supposed was intended tact,

'It's a formal affair and the ladies usually wear sleeveless gowns on such occasions. Have you one? I ask this because I notice you favour dresses with sleeves.'

'They're only short sleeves.' She had gone a trifle pale. The scar on her shoulder was not a pretty sight. 'I prefer a small sleeve,' she added, never dreaming at this stage that he would carry the matter further.

'It will please me if you wear the correct dress for the occasion,' he said in tones as quiet as her own but decidedly inflexible.

She shook her head.

'I can't—I'm uncomfortable——'

'Nonsense! If you haven't one I'll give you the money and you can go into town and get one.'

Again she shook her head.

'I can't,' she repeated desperately. 'Surely I'm allowed to wear what I like?' Was he considering her to be obstinate? she wondered, loath to give him a reason for this argument on her part. He never tolerated anything inferior . . . . Morag's words came back and Gail added with sudden firmness, 'I must wear what I like, Andrew—what I feel most comfortable in.'

'You'll observe my wishes,' he snapped, and left her,

returning a few minutes later ,with an open cheque in his hand. 'Get what you want, but make sure it's sleeveless,' he added darkly, and placed the cheque on the table.

Of course she pleased herself and wore a dress with short sleeves, but as she had on a wrap he did not learn of Gail's disregard of his wishes until they arrived at the ball. She came down from the magnificent powder room to meet his smouldering and astounded gaze. All the other women were in sleeveless gowns, many with the narrowest of shoulder-straps; Gail naturally felt different, but this was preferable to revealing her unsightly disfigurement.

'How dare you disobey me?' he hissed when presently he managed to speak without being overheard, 'How dare you!'

It was the first time the real barb of his temper had been directed at her and Gail's face went white.

'I'm sorry,' she faltered, 'but I couldn't. I'm far happier like this.' Had he asked her the reason she felt she would have told him, so unhappy did she feel at his anger. But he did not ask her and she knew for sure that he was considering her to be merely obstinate—just like his first wife had been, and his daughter was being all the time. During the whole evening she was conscious of his fury, suppressed when necessary but very plainly revealed in the glowering looks he gave her on the occasions when they got up to dance together. His words he kept until they were driving home in the car; she was then subjected to a little of what his errant daughter had so many times deservedly experienced. Gail remained dumb, in spite of her mounting resentment of his attitude, but her silence infuriated him and on entering the house he rounded on her, his smouldering gaze once again causing the colour to drain from her face.

'Don't you ever dare defy me like that again,' he threatened, 'or by heaven you'll regret it!'

'I do not consider it in the light of defiance,' she

82

managed to say, although not in very steady tones. 'I have a right to please myself what I wear.'

'Not if I am to be disgraced—as I was this evening!'

Disgraced? No one had paid especial attention to her gown. Could it have been that good manners forbade it, though? Would the comments and deprecations be passed around at tomorrow's inevitable coffee mornings? Gail had never throught of that, and perhaps, it was as well, for her discomfiture was great enough without the added anxiety of what the fashionable throng was thinking about her. It was her first important ball and the way she felt at present she hoped it would be a long while before she was forced to attend another.

'I'm sorry if you feel I disgraced you,' she began when he wrathfully cut her short.

'I don't feel, as you term it, I know! It was pure obstinacy on your part, for there's no reason at all why you shouldn't have worn a suitable gown——'

'You don't know if it was obstinacy,' she interrupted, having decided to tell him the truth and put an end to this painful scene. 'As a matter of fact——'

'I do know it was obstinacy,' he thundered. 'Because that's a trait of all women!'

Her eyes suddenly glinted. She forgot for a moment what he had suffered and remembered only the injustice of his treatment of her on so many occasions. She would not be made the scapegoat like this.

'You judge all women the same, then?' she asked, but gave him no opportunity to reply as she went on, her voice quivering with anger, her temper forming a hard little lump in her throat. 'You've not known me long enough to judge me, or to learn of any traits I possess, so don't be so quick to jump to conclusions! However, whether you choose to consider it obstinacy or not, I shall continue to wear what suits me, and if my choice doesn't happen to coincide with your ideas of what's correct then that's just too bad!'

An astounded silence followed. Up till now she had

been so obliging and amenable that he had probably taken it for granted she did not possess a temper. His own temper had died when at length he spoke, but his words had by no means lost their sting.

'Just let me give you some good advice, Gail. Don't run away with the idea that because Morag defies me you can do the same. She's ungovernable simply because she's immune to hurt. But you don't possess her insensibility; she's invulnerable—you're not. Flaunt my authority and you'll be hurt—hurt so you'll remember it for a long while. Take the advice I'm offering,' he continued in a very soft tone, his blue eyes never leaving her face, 'and observe my wishes—because you'll find life more than a little unpleasant if you don't.'

His words were with her all night, because she scarcely slept. They revealed much—his complete understanding of both Morag's character and her own. Gail had asserted in her temper that he had not known her long enough to have become aware of any outstanding traits she possessed, but she now admitted she was wrong. He had stated firmly that she was vulnerable ... but did he know just how vulnerable? Gail herself was only just beginning to ask that question. The answer remained elusive, perhaps owing to Gail's continued shirking of any deep analysis of her feelings where Andrew was concerned.

One thing Gail did have to admit: Morag's sneering references to Gail's falling in love with her husband remained long after they were uttered detracting exceedingly from Gail's peace of mind.

The balmy April spring melted imperceptibly into the glory of May, and the danger of any real inclemency in the weather was passed. The atmosphere within the house was, however, still fraught with icy tension, and Gail actually experienced a certain relief when Andrew announced his intention of spending a fortnight on his estate further north. It was during his absence that she met Robin Sheldon, a stocky but handsome young man whose parents had sold their business in England and made an early retirement, coming to live in a pretty little cottage nestling in the hills above the village. Mrs. Sheldon was a Scot from Perth and Robin himself had been working in that city for some time, living with an aunt and going home to his parents only in holiday times. He had met Gail on the road when, having a flat tyre, Gail had done the obvious feminine thing—stood looking helplessly at her wheel, but with one eye expectantly on all passing cars as she awaited the inevitable chivalrous driver who would come to her aid.

'What's up?' Robin had asked after steering his car on to the verge.

'A puncture. I suppose I should be able to change the wheel, but. . . .' She smiled at him and within minutes he was changing the wheel for her, glancing up now and then to admire her lovely slender figure and the rare beauty of her face.

'There! Done in a crack!'

'Thank you very much,' she said gratefully. 'I must get my husband or someone to show me what to do, just in case I have another puncture some time.'

'Husband?' He glanced at her left hand. 'Oh, well, it's just my luck,' he said good-humouredly, and Gail laughed.

They met again as Gail and the children came out of church the following Sunday.

'Are these your children?' he asked after he and Gail had smilingly greeted one another.

'They're my stepchildren—Robbie and Shena.'

He looked curiously at her. 'Where do you live?'

She pointed to the great mansion high on the hill. 'That's my home.'

'Dunlochrie House. . . .' Again he looked curiously at her. 'There's another girl,' he said slowly, and Gail nodded, aware that he knew all about Morag and her wild escapades. Her heart went out to her husband.

85

How he must deplore the publicity! Deep contrition swept over her; bitterly she regretted that scene, caused entirely by her own disinclination to provide Andrew with a reason for her disregard of his request that she wear a sleeveless evening gown. She should not have caused him unnecessary annoyance and added hurt. Hurt? Could he be hurt? she wondered, and suddenly recalled her conviction that a heart did in fact beat beneath that armour of hard inflexibility.

The moment he returned, she decided, she would tell him about the accident, and the scars she carried on her body. He would understand then, and readily forgive her.

'Is Morag home at present?' inquired Robin as they walked together out of the churchyard to where both their cars were parked.

'Yes, she's at home.' The brief answer warned him that Gail was not inclined to discuss the recalcitrant daughter of the Laird of Dunlochrie, and yet he added,

'She goes away quite a lot, I understand?'

'She has many friends; naturally she visits them. It's quiet here for a young girl.'

'She should be at school still.' They had reached Gail's car and the children were already getting into the back seat. Gail looked straight at him.

'That's her father's affair. I never discuss such things with anyone.'

He shrugged, looking up to the big house, stately and impressive in the light of the brilliant May morning. Silhouetted against the blue sky, away in the far distance, was the herd of roe deer, grazing on the heather-clad ridge, with along to the left the silver ribbon of a tumbling burn as it sped on its way to join the valley of the Tilt.

'Your husband doesn't come to church?' he said as if in an effort to delay her as she slid into the car.

'He's away at present, but he usually comes to church with us.' She closed the door but let the window down. 'I haven't seen you at church before.'

Robin grimaced.

'I don't come often. Only did it this morning because it was something to do. One becomes bored around here.'

'Your parents like it, though?'

'Mother's a Scot; she always intended retiring to this particular village. She was born hereabouts, but her parents moved to Perth when she was small. They often visited their friends and Mother grew to love this district.'

Gail pressed the starter.

'I could do with some fishing,' he said with strange urgency. 'Can I come up to the loch?'

'The loch? I don't know if my husband allows it.'

'You don't know?' He raised his brows ... and again she saw that curious look appear on his handsome face. But all he said was, 'I've heard he does allow fishing in the loch. Shall I come up and see his factor?'

She was in a quandary, not having heard anything of this permission of which Robin spoke.

'I suppose there isn't any reason why you shouldn't see Mr. Sinclair.'

'Fine. I'll be up this afternoon. See you later,' he added quickly as Gail let in the clutch. She said good-bye and drove away, a strange uneasiness enveloping her and remaining undispelled even by the incessant chatter of the children.

Robin appeared at two o'clock. Mrs. Birchan opened the door and he asked for Gail. The housekeeper showed him into the sitting-room where Gail was putting on Robbie's coat and scarf.

'Oh. ...' She was taken aback. 'You want to see Mr. Sinclair. I'll send for him.' Mrs. Birchan had gone and Gail rang the bell. One of the maids came and Gail asked her to fetch the estate manager.

'You're going out?' Robin took possession of the chair Gail indicated as she invited him to sit down.

'We always go for a ramble on Sunday afternoons,' put in Robbie before she could answer. 'Daddy comes too, but he isn't here today. Do you want to come with us?'

The young man glanced at Gail before speaking to Robbie.

'Would you like me to?'

'Yes——' Robbie also glanced at Gail. 'If Mummy wants you to.'

'Mr. Sheldon has come to do some fishing,' said Gail with undue haste, turning her head as Sinclair entered the room. She introduced him to Robin, who then made his request.

'Mummy, I can't find my gloves.' Shena already had on her outdoor clothes—a bright red coat and hat, both trimmed with fur. 'I put them in my pocket, but they're not there now.'

'They're on the hall table,' Gail told her, and she ran from the room to fetch them.

Sinclair had requested Robin to follow him to his office and reluctantly he also left the room, smiling at Gail as he passed her.

The permission was granted and as Gail and the children came out of the house Robin was taking his fishing tackle from the car, which he had driven on to the forecourt.

'The loch's some distance from here,' Gail told him. 'You'd better take the car; the road goes quite close to the loch.'

'The walk will do me good.' He paused uncertainly. 'You don't mind if I come with you?'

A small hesitation and then,

'I hadn't decided to go that way.'

'Oh, but we nearly always go to the loch,' interposed Robbie eagerly. 'I'd like to go there, and we can see Mr. Sheldon catch some fish.'

Bank fishing was not allowed; Gail had heard that mentioned one day when Andew was on the phone, but at the time she had not been particularly interested and, therefore, had not asked about it.

'You won't see him catch any fish, Robbie, because

88

he'll be in the boat.'

'Well, let's walk with Mr. Sheldon,' persisted Robbie. 'And we can see him getting into the boat.'

'Yes, let's,' put in Shena, but still Gail hesitated. Why had her uneasiness returned? There was no accounting for it and presently she shook it off, smiling at Shena and agreeing to walk with Robin to the loch.

CHAPTER SIX

THEY left Robin at the loch and rambled as usual over the grouse moors towards the burn. With the mildness of the spring new growth was appearing all around, while on the lower arable land which constituted only a minute portion of the vast estate the tender green shoots of barley and rye made a carpet of velvet that would surely attract the deer before very long. Gunshots in the air would scare them on to the higher hill grazing where the food was less delectable but the situation far more safe.

The hills and glens and tumbling burns, the stark crags of the mountains and wild solitude of the moors, the cry of a grouse or trill of a ring-ouzel at dawn ... all had contributed to the spell which Gail's new environment had cast upon her. She loved the frosty mornings when the air intoxicated, the warm afternoons when the pale yellow sunlight softened the peaks and sprayed shadows into the glens; she loved the silence and the shade of gloaming and the clear, star-spangled sky at night. She had been lucky, Sinclair told her, for this particular year was exceptional. Wait until we had a real hard spring, he had warned ... and as for the severity of winter in the Highlands....

But Gail was not alarmed, nor even remotely troubled; in England each season had held its own particular charms for her and she had no doubts that the same would happen here.

'Mummy ... hush, there are some baby foxes playing down there, by that cairn. Can you see them?'

'Yes.' They all stopped and Gail wished she had a stalking-glass. For the vixen and her cubs were a long way off and all that could be discerned was the rich red streak of the mother and the two darker bundles of fur that were her cubs.

'We must tell Daddy and then he can have them shot.' Shena put a warm little gloved hand in Gail's as she spoke and Gail frowned momentarily. The cubs looked so very sweet. . . .

'I'll bet that vixen had the lamb Meredith found near another cairn,' said Robbie, squatting down as if for a more productive view. 'I heard him telling Daddy that a vixen had moved her den when the terriers killed two of her cubs. Meredith was out all night trying to find the new den, and he was *so* cold and wet when he did come in!'

Gail heaved a deep sigh. This was the harsh reality of the Scottish Highlands. A dog or vixen in their dire need to rear their cubs would often resort to killing lambs and there was nothing to be done except keep their numbers down. There was no danger of the foxes disappearing altogether, Andrew had assured her, but, looking down to where the enchanting little creatures frolicked, all oblivious of their probable fate, she derived scant satisfaction from her husband's words.

'It's getting dark,' said Robbie suddenly. 'I think it's going to rain.'

Rain was certainly in the air now; the heights of Ben-y-Gloe and the neighbouring mountains were becoming indeterminate in the oncoming shadows cast by the low and scudding clouds.

'We must go back,' decided Gail at once, with a quick thought for Robin who was probably still in the middle of the loch.

Mrs. Davis's car was on the forecourt as they reached the house; she and Morag were having tea by the fire in the small sitting-room where a log fire burned cheerfully in the grate, its high flames complementing the light given off by the rose-shaded standard lamp in the corner of the room.

The two stopped talking abruptly as Gail and the children entered, all their faces flushed and shining from their brisk walk which had been necessary to beat the rain. On entering the hall both children had slipped their hands into those of Gail, and their grandmother noticed this as they all three stood there, Gail's face portraying faint inquiry and surprise.

'I'm sorry we were out,' she murmured apologetically. 'You don't usually call on Sundays.'

'Not when Andrew's at home, no.' The familiar disdainful glance for Gail and a smile for the children and then, 'He likes his week-ends to himself.' The words implied much more than was said—unsociableness, for one thing—but Gail offered no excuse for her husband's natural desire for privacy and relaxation after five exhausting days spent on the estate.

'If you'd rung,' she said, unbuttoning Shena's coat, 'I'd not have taken the children out.'

'We've been quite cosy, here on our own.' In Morag's hard eyes was a strange mingling of interest and curiosity, but it was not until the departure of Mrs. Davis half an hour later that Gail learned the reason for it. The children had gone to wash their hands before tea and Gail was sitting by the fire, having rung for the maid and told her they were ready. Normally Gail made the children's tea herself, but on Sunday she must have a rest, Andrew had said in one of his rare moments of armour-free concern for her.

'Who's your boy-friend?' asked Morag as soon as the door closed behind the maid.

Gail glanced up haughtily.

'I'm afraid I don't understand?'

'Is he the one who bought you the flowers?' Reaching for the solitary sandwich remaining on the plate, Morag bit into it, impervious to the frigidity of the atmosphere resulting from her first question.

'I've known Mr. Sheldon only a few days!'

'Then he must be a fast worker, coming to call on you like that—oh, yes, I saw him, and watched you go off walking with him.' She nibbled at the bread and added, 'Do you have clandestine meetings? I rather think that must be fun,' she went on, diverted. 'Hmm. . . .' Morag looked reflectively into the fire.

'Maybe I shall decide to marry after all because it must be exciting having someone to pit your wits against. Yes, a husband would provide the barrier it would be daring to scale. One would have a sense of achievement, of victory!' Gail's eyes flicked her contemptuously, but Morag only laughed, throwing the bread back on to the plate so carelessly that it went on to the floor. She made no attempt to pick it up as she said, 'You'll be in trouble if Father finds out about your boyfriend because he'll conclude that history's repeating itself. Mother had men-friends—but you know that.'

Revulsion sweeping over her, Gail rose and left the room, going along to the kitchen to inform the maid that they would be having their tea in the snug.

A short while after his return Andrew sought Gail out in the nursery where she was tidying up the cupboards, having already sorted out the games which the children had got mixed up, and putting them in their appropriate boxes.

'Who's the man you've had up here?' he demanded wrathfully, startling her into speechlessness for a moment. She knew from where his information had come, but she said slowly,

'You've been speaking to Sinclair?'

'I've been speaking to Morag,' he rapped out, while at the same time frowning at her question. She did not answer at once but looked up at him, recalling her determination to put things right between them by telling him the reason for her refusal to wear a dress of his liking. But as she took in the attitude of cold mastery and accusation all her good intentions fled and the angry colour mounted her cheeks.

'Perhaps,' she invited, for the moment retaining her control, 'you'll tell me exactly what she said?'

He hesitated and she became a trifle breathless. Had he continued to show reluctance Gail would undoubtedly have phrased a satisfactory explanation, but he said furiously at last,

93

'She said you were out walking with him on Sunday afternoon——'

'With the children? Did she tell you the children were with me?' He nodded, his mouth tight, and she went on, 'He came to my assistance when I had a puncture——'

'Puncture? How convenient!' His voice snapped, ice-edged.

Gail's temper lodged in her throat, suffocatingly.

'The next time I saw him,' she continued with admirable calm, 'was on coming out of church. He asked me about a permit to fish in the loch here.'

'He did?—on so brief an acquaintanceship?' She did not speak and he went on, 'You gave him permission to fish in the loch?' Again that icy edge to his voice, but the rein on her temper was firm—as yet.

'I referred him to Sinclair—a course which, I believe, was the correct one to take.'

A movement in Andrew's throat was the only sign of emotion now as he said, very softly,

'Be careful, Gail. Remember whom you are speaking to.' Automatically she lowered her head and he went on to say, 'Did Sinclair give your friend permission to fish in the loch?'

'My friend? He gave Mr. Sheldon permission to fish. That's why we were walking with him; the children wanted to and I agreed.'

'The children?' he repeated, raising his brows.

Lifting her head, she looked squarely at him.

'Yes, Andrew, the children.'

Hard eyes roved over her; she wondered if he were thinking about his late wife and, as Morag had mentioned, feeling history was repeating itself.

'I'll see Sinclair. This man won't come here again. And you will not speak to him again, understand?'

Unleashed at last, her temper flared.

'I do *not* understand! Morag has her own ideas about my relationship with Robin—with Mr. Sheldon,' she amended as his face darkened. 'And she appears to have conveyed those ideas to you. If you like to believe her then do so by all means, I have no control over your suspicions. But as for not speaking to Mr. Sheldon—I'll please myself! What would you have me do—cut him dead the next time we meet? Is that what you mean?'

'That's exactly what I mean.'

'Then you're in for a disappointment! My good manners won't allow me to treat him in so ungracious a way!'

He advanced upon her, tall and masculine, with dark fury in his eyes. Gail stepped back, pale now and trembling, a hand unconsciously going to her head. The scar had swelled above her throbbing temple. The wall stopped further backward progress and Andrew came threateningly close.

'I'm in for a disappointment, am I?' His voice was dangerously low as he added, 'Should I be disappointed, Gail, then believe me you'll be exceedingly sorry for yourself!'

Her heart raced painfully—fear, to her surprise, rising above her temper. For there was a ruthlessness about him she had never seen before. It was as if all the savagery of a bygone age were depicted in his features, giving them a cruel, almost satanic appearance.

Was he threatening her with violence? she wondered.

'We'll wait and see whether or not I'm to be sorry for myself,' she managed to say quietly at last.

'You intend to defy me?'

'I intend to treat Mr. Sheldon in the way good manners demand.'

'You'll not speak to him again!' he thundered, white lines appearing at the sides of his mouth. 'I'm ordering you to ignore him, no matter in what circumstances you happen to meet!'

Her legs felt weak, and every nerve in her body fluttered. Unbridled fury such as this she had never visualized when with such sublime optimism she had consented to marry him. Heather had disliked him, prophesying that Gail would be making a hash of her life. What would Heather think should she ever witness a scene like this? Gail's eyes pricked, yet frightened as she now was she refused to capitulate, knowing full well she could never treat Robin in the way Andrew had just ordered her to do.

'Andrew ... I can't cut him, f-for no reason at all——' The rest died on her lips as her husband reached out and, taking a vicious hold on her arms, shook her till the tears started to her eyes. But suddenly he paused, his hands sliding down her arms, stopping only when they reached her wrists, where they remained, as he stared at her, his blue eyes fixed and disbelieving.

'That scar,' he said at last, as if the words were dragged from him. 'How did you get it?'

She shook her head, drained and weak and wishing in her moment of abject misery that she had never set eyes on him.

'It was—it was——' pulling herself free, she put her hands to her face and wept.

'Gail....' He sounded stunned, and contrite, and gentle all at once. 'My dear, don't cry. I'm sorry I hurt you....' And before either of them realized what was happening she was in his arms and she felt his lips touching the scar she had tried so hard to conceal from him. 'Tell me about it,' he encouraged softly. 'What happened?'

But all Gail could do for the moment was lift her head from his chest and stare, wide-eyed and breathless, as she tried to assimilate this sudden change in him. He was looking at the scar; it was pulsating and livid because of the emotional disturbance through which she had just passed.

'I was in a car crash,' she whispered presently. 'I have another, much more unsightly, scar on my shoulder——'

'Your shoulder?' sharply, as a paleness touched his

mouth, but for an altogether different reason this time. 'That was why you wouldn't——?' He stopped, because she was already nodding her head. 'Gail, you silly girl. Why didn't you tell me?'

She remembered once again Morag's words about his not tolerating anything inferior and knew she couldn't tell him about the other scars on her body. Later, perhaps—although it wasn't necessary because he would never see them.... Never? Why had her heart leapt just then? Why, for that matter, was he holding her like this, and looking at her with softened eyes, touching her with hands so gentle that she could scarcely believe in the hurt they had so recently inflicted?

'I wanted to, but I expect it was just stubbornness on my part—afterwards, that was,' she went on to explain, though not very effectively because he said,

'Afterwards?' and looked questioningly at her.

'At first I didn't want you to know about my scars,' she confessed, and bent her head, confused, as he looked at her with an odd expression.

'You didn't want me to know? But why?'

She would not repeat what Morag had said, naturally.

'I had an idea you disliked anything inferior.'

'And you considered yourself inferior?' Andrew gave her no opportunity of answering that as he went on to chide her, but in a very different way from his former harsh and dominating manner of approach. 'What gave you the idea I disliked anything inferior?' he queried as an afterthought.

'One gets—impressions,' was all she said, and to her relief he pursued the matter no further, merely shaking his head in a bewildered sort of way as if unable to understand why she should have reached a conclusion like that.

She dried her cheeks and smiled, calmed now by his gentleness and the way he had passed over the matter of her disfigurement as if it was of no account. To think she had worried and fretted, wishing so many times

97

recently that she had entered hospital long ago and had something done about those scars. It was over two years, she recalled, since the doctor had first told her she need no longer carry her disfigurements.

'Can I tell you about Robin?' she ventured after a while, not only because she felt he was in a receptive mood but also because the nearness of him was soothing and pleasant and she had no wish to move away. He had held her close a moment ago, and touched her temple with his lips . . . and Gail wished she knew of a way of making him do the same again.

'Yes,' he returned in the same soft and gentle tones. 'Come and sit down on the couch and tell me everything.'

It was in fact little different from what she had already told him, but in his new and tolerant mood of patience and understanding he saw the whole situation as it really was and not through the distorted vision of anger and mistrust.

'I'm sorry, Gail,' he said at last. 'My only excuse is that——' He stopped, his eyes brooding and dark. 'I can't speak of it, but there was an excuse, believe me.' He smiled at her and her pulse fluttered. How changed his expression . . . how attractive he was!

The incident brought them closer, one aspect of the change in Andrew being that he invariably joined Gail and the children for tea in the afternoons. It was always a cosy, intimate situation and one to which they all looked forward. The Sunday afternoon walks continued and on the odd occasion, when he wasn't too busy, Andrew would accompany Gail when she went to pick up the children from school. Gail and Andrew began visiting in the evenings; she knew that remarks were passed in her favour and that Andrew's friends were relieved that at last some happiness had been brought into his life. They themselves gave dinner parties in the great tapestry-hung dining-room which would glitter with silver and cut-glass and the jewels worn by the ladies.

But of course Morag was still to be reckoned with—being a barrier to Andrew's peace of mind and as great an annoyance to Gail as she could possibly make herself. A bitter quarrel between Morag and Andrew would always mean the return of his black mood. Gail would speculate on his thoughts at these times, wondering if he suspected Morag was not his, and if so, whether he was fiercely resentful that she should be plaguing him like this. But he seemed all the while to be drawing closer to Gail and to be deriving comfort from her. A sign of the new relationship developing between them was the way in which he would discuss Morag with his wife.

'I'm thinking of sending her to boarding school,' he mentioned one day when he and Gail were alone in the snug. He omitted to mention the two previous expulsions and Gail naturally made no attempt to inform him of what she had overheard.

'You have a school in mind?' she asked cautiously.

'There are two—one near Edinburgh and one in England. I'll write to them both.'

The one in Edinburgh would not take Morag, the Principal no doubt having a knowledge of the girl's record. There being no such bar with the school in England it was arranged that Morag should start in September. Whether or not she would go was a matter for conjecture, and if she did consent to go, whether or not she would stay remained to be seen.

It would be heaven without her, Gail had to admit, often recalling her own optimism about being able to do something for Morag. She had failed, very early admitting that nothing could be done for the girl. She had had her sixteenth birthday recently; Gail bought her a silver brush and comb set for her dressing table, having ascertained by subtle questioning that she hadn't one, a circumstance that surprised Gail but made her choice of a present much easier. Gail also made Robbie and Shena buy presents for their sister. All of these Gail showed to Andrew, having overheard him telling Morag she would receive nothing from him.

'What are you giving her?' Gail tentatively asked, hoping to force him into buying a present for Morag.

'I've told her she's getting nothing.' He obligingly examined the presents, his eyes glinting angrily as he looked at the brush and comb set, but it wasn't until she presented her gift that Gail learned the reason for this.

'I'd have found more use for cigarettes,' said Morag ungratefully on opening the parcel. 'However, I can sell this, as I sold the other. Thanks, anyway.'

'You've sold one?'

'Father gave me a set when he was in one of his generous moods—an antique thing that had been in the family for generations. Then he became so stingy with money that I had to sell it.'

Despite her anger at Morag's reception of her gift Gail could not help pitying her, for she was missing so much in life.

Could she be wholly blamed for what she was? The world of nature was largely cut and dried. To a certain degree one was capable of shaping one's own character, it was true, because instinctively one was able to differentiate between right and wrong, but many characteristics were inherent, determined by those often troublesome little things called genes. They were the basic units of heredity and, therefore, largely responsible for a person's character and appearance. Normally a man passed much of what was in himself on to his female offspring, but there was nothing of Andrew in Morag ... nothing at all. And that was why Gail pitied her. If Andrew was not her father then the loss was hers.

At the beginning of July she went off again to visit friends, leaving a note for Andrew saying she would be away three weeks. There was no address, no indication as to whether she had any money—although Gail felt she could not have much and, therefore, could not have gone abroad. To Gail's surprise Andrew appeared disinterested, his only sign of temper being the tearing across of the note and the tossing of it into the waste-paper basket.

Shortly after that Robin came; Gail had seen him only twice since that unhappy scene with Andrew and now she looked anxiously at her husband, fearing he would be in an unapproachable mood after having received the note Morag had left him. But he received Robin cordially enough, giving him permission to fish, and much later Gail saw them talking together by Robin's car, just before the young man went home.

A few days after Morag's departure Andrew asked Gail if she would like Heather and Roger to come for a holiday. The suggestion came as a complete surprise and Gail was naturally delighted. But, aware of her sister's dislike of Andrew, and remembering that she had once refused a similar invitation, she did have slight misgivings as she wrote the invitation. From the first, letters had passed between them, with Heather always putting anxious questions and Gail sending reassuring replies. She was perfectly happy, she had always maintained, feeling no compunction at the white lies, designed as they were to relieve Heather of unnecessary anxiety. Beth had also put questions, though more tentatively and not as often. It was not because she loved Gail less than Heather did, but because, having met Andrew for the first time at the wedding, and on that occasion only briefly, she had not had the opportunity of forming an impression of her brother-in-law.

'Could Beth and her family come later?' Gail had asked, and immediately Andrew had suggested they all come together.

'It would be a nice family reunion for you,' he smiled, but Gail had wondered if it would be too much for the servants.

'There would be four extra children,' she ended, but again her husband only smiled.

'The servants can manage,' he said, and to Gail's delight both her sisters accepted the invitations and they all arrived together in two cars.

Thomas and Marilyn already knew Andrew's children and immediately rushed off with them to the swings. Simon and Manda stayed shyly by their parents, looking up at the trophies with awe and wonderment in their eyes. Gail called to Robbie, who came at once.

'This is Simon and Manda,' she said. 'They also want to play.'

'Come on, then,' said Robert in a hurry. 'I'll race you to the swings!'

Two maids had appeared to take the luggage upstairs, but Gail herself led the way, showing Beth her room first, with the children's rooms just across the passage.

'I'll see you downstairs,' she said, and then took Heather along to three similar rooms.

'What happened to the men?' Heather wanted to know.

'They've gone to have a drink.' Gail turned. 'Leave the cases there, please, Dora. I'll help my sister to unpack.' The girl put down the suitcases and left the room.

'Still the same,' commented Heather a trifle disparagingly. 'Andrew prefers men's company.'

'He did ask you and Beth to join them when you were ready,' returned Gail with unaccustomed crispness. 'But you were so busy talking to me you didn't hear him.'

Heather looked strangely at her, examining her face.

'Touchy, aren't we?' she said, though with a hint of amusement. 'You're not falling in love with that brute, I hope.'

'Do you like your rooms?' inquired Gail, putting one of the suitcases on a chair and opening the lid.

'Avoiding the question, eh? Yes, they're magnificent —and the view from here! Those mountains and

102

moors! And that blue sky! I thought it always rained in Scotland.'

'So did I. But this year's been exceptional. We've had no snow at all—only on the high mountains further north, and on a few here. Ben-y-Gloe had snow on it until about a month ago.'

'Which is Ben-y-Gloe?'

'That one—between those other two. It's also called the Mountain of the Mist.'

'Well, there's no mist on it now. I think we're going to have marvellous weather. I'm glad you asked us to come, Gail.'

'I'm glad you came. I had a feeling you might refuse.'

'Not this time, because you're here.' She looked round. 'You certainly married money—which is some compensation for what you're missing,' she added bluntly. Gail made no comment on that and Heather added, eyeing her curiously, 'Morag. . . .? You're always so evasive over my questions. I'm dying to meet her.'

'You won't; she's away visiting friends. Shall I unpack this case for you?'

Heather nodded and said,

'Away visiting friends?' She paused. 'On one of her escapades, you mean?'

'I expect so,' shrugged Gail, and again changed the subject. 'We're having a barbecue on Thursday—if the weather stays like this.'

Heather looked perceptively at her, but was not to be put off.

'I expect you arranged this visit because she was away?'

'Andrew made the suggestion,' she returned noncommittally, but Heather merely smiled.

'Does she give you a bad time? I mean—she must resent you.'

'We do have our clashes,' admitted Gail. 'But on the whole I have little to do with her.'

'So your good resolutions came unstuck? You

103

haven't managed to reform her?'

Taking out one of her sister's dresses, Gail hung it in the wardrobe. When she turned again Heather was still waiting for an answer.

'I hate to admit it, but——' Gail shook her head. 'It's an awful thing to say, Heather, but I don't think Morag can be reformed.'

'If she manages to get herself a decent husband?'

Gail sighed, thinking of what Morag had said about the fun and excitement of deceiving a husband.

'I should imagine decent young men give her a wide berth.'

Heather began to unpack her other suitcase.

'The two small ones ... how about them? They seemed tractable enough when I had them.'

'They're wonderful children.' Her eyes brightened, revealing her inner animation and enthusiasm. 'I love them dearly—and they love me, so I'm very lucky indeed.'

'So you've got what you wanted—and I must say it would have been a waste if someone like you hadn't had the upbringing of children. I'm glad for you, Gail, really happy that your desire materialized.' And then she added, on noting the swift, unintentional change in Gail's expression, 'Andrew ...?' No answer from Gail and Heather went on slowly, 'I hinted that you might be falling in love with him...?'

Gail flushed and nodded reluctantly.

'Yes,' she admitted, because she and Heather had never had secrets from one another. 'I find myself caring much more than is good for my peace of mind.'

'A *contretemps* you didn't reckon with?'

Gail frowned.

'I wouldn't call it that——'

'You wouldn't?' interrupted Heather quickly. 'You mean he's falling in love too?' And yet she shook her head. 'He's too hard, Gail. He couldn't fall in love.'

Gail had to laugh, even though her thoughts were serious as she recalled her husband's softness and contrition after hurting her because of his suspicions about Robin.

'You've formed your own picture of him, haven't you?'

'He was so arrogant and pompous on every occasion I had the misfortune—I mean,' she amended, remembering she was now a guest in Andrew's house, 'on every occasion I met him. And you know yourself he could scarcely bear to speak to either of us when you came on that last visit.'

Gail opened a drawer and laid Heather's underwear in it.

'He did speak to me, though. He asked me to marry him.' She glanced up, amusement in her eyes. 'Seriously, Heather, he isn't like that at all. He's been through a lot—much more than most men of his age, and if it's made him a little hard and bitter no one can blame him. Underneath he's tolerant and understanding, and—and I think he could fall in love. . . .' Yet she tailed off, her eyes clouding. Was she living in a fool's paradise?

'I hope,' said Heather angrily, 'that you're not in for another hurt.'

'Andrew's been much more human lately, and if it weren't for Morag—— She makes him so angry and then he's sharp and impatient with everyone.' Closing the drawer, Gail straightened up. 'Time will tell, I suppose. We haven't been married very long and, after all, I haven't been deceived in any way, or misled. Andrew gave me to understand there'd be nothing in the marriage, and I agreed because that was what I wanted—at the time.'

'It's not natural for you to go on like this. You're normal—and a man like Andrew must have all the normal desires, too. Does he go out much?' Heather suddenly asked, frowning. 'On his own, I mean?'

'He doesn't have women friends, if that's what you're suggesting!'

'Sorry, I didn't mean to hurt you. No, I don't believe

he would have women friends—not of that sort.' Heather changed the subject then and at last Gail received all the news for which she had been waiting.

Roger had landed a big contract, and his firm was in the running for another; Marilyn had won a silver medal for her dancing, making five in all. Simon had found a dead pheasant on the front lawn and everyone except Roger had cried. . . .

Beth's news was imparted a short while later when they were in the sitting-room with the men. Andrew occasionally cocked an ear, interestedly watching his wife's face and smiling at her whenever she happened to catch his eye. She was inordinately happy to be entertaining her family like this, for always she had been the guest, having no home of her own. And later, when the children came rushing in, flushed and hungry, addressing her as Mummy as if they had been doing so all their lives, she really felt her cup to be full as she firmly set aside her more intimate desires and took what was there, well within her reach.

'Mummy . . . oh, I must have something to eat!' gasped Robbie.

'So must I!' Shena was almost as breathless as her brother.

'We're all hungry,' put in Thomas, more sedately, being older. 'Can we have some sandwiches, please, Auntie Gail?'

'I think tea will be ready,' put in Andrew, reaching for the bell-rope. Dora appeared almost at once and in answer to his question said the tea would be ready in five minutes' time.

They all sat down together—the six adults at one table and the children at another. It was a noisy meal, but no one cared, and Gail saw her husband as the family man, congenial and relaxed, yet not losing his inherent dignity.

'I like your husband,' whispered Beth, on making sure Andrew could not hear. 'Where did Heather get the idea that he was awful?'

'She didn't know him very well.'

'It's a wonder you don't fall in love with him.'

'I have. Can I help you to more scones?'

'You have! But, Gail, you chump!'

'The butter's to your left. Would you like more tea?'

'Will he fall for you, do you think?'

'He might—if my stars up there just keep going in their present direction.'

'But supposing he doesn't?' said Beth anxiously.

'I have the children.' But her voice faltered. On losing Michael Gail's one desire had been to be with children; vaguely she had known she must one day work with them and that encounter in the park had decided things for her. She would change her job after the holiday with Heather, and she had firmly believed then that children would be enough. On accepting Andrew's proposal she had again believed children would be enough, felt sure that although she desired to be a wife as well as a mother, a 'wife in name only' position would have satisfied her. It would, had she not felt like this about Andrew, but she did feel like this ... and now she knew that fulfilment did not come with children alone. Was she asking too much? she wondered fearfully. The fates had been kind, lifting her from her lonely spinster status and giving her two wonderful children, a home of which to be proud, and a husband who was far far above the ordinary run of men. Should she be satisfied?—grateful for the bounties received, asking for no more?

'Does Andrew know—everything?' asked Beth a trifle hesitantly as Gail refilled her teacup.

'He knows about the accident. He saw the scar on my head and asked about it, so I had to tell him I'd been in a crash. He doesn't know anything else.' Her voice faded as another thought struck her. Supposing Andrew did fall in love with her ... would he expect to have more children? The idea frightened her, and she put it out of her mind, turning to speak to Roger, and then joining in the general conversation going on around her.

To her surprise, and also to her intense satisfaction, Andrew decided not to work at all while their visitors were with them. He needed the rest, she thought, and as it was to coincide with Morag's absence there would be nothing to prevent his obtaining the maximum benefit of both physical rest and mental relaxation.

It was a typical country holiday, spent mainly out of doors, for the weather remained fine and sunny and on several days it was hot enough to sunbathe on the lawn, all except Gail in the scantiest of attire. The swimming pool was put to good use, as was the putting green which had been made only the year before on part of the lawn at one side of the house.

Rambling over the moors or in the glen, watching nature, was a delight shared by all, even though much was missed because of the inability of the children to make a silent approach when something interesting was happening.

They were thrilled with the roe deer but could not get close enough for their liking, and would often give disappointed little cries as, after 'stalking' the deer, they would then see them take off, making their gazelle-like bounds towards a rise, over which they would disappear from sight.

Andrew was continually plied with questions by the children of his sisters-in-law, and always he answered with patience, for he himself took a keen interest in all that went on around him.

All predatory birds left the nest in July, from the great golden eagle to the relatively small sparrowhawk. But as they did not immediately fend for themselves they could sometimes be seen—if the children could be persuaded to go quietly—being fed by their parents.

Sometimes the birds would be seen over the grouse moors, looking for prey—buzzards and kestrels and peregrine falcons. The eagles were never seen feeding their young because their eyries were high on some cliff and one had to climb in order to get close enough.

'Have you seen them feeding, Uncle Andrew?' Manda wanted to know. Having taken a particular liking to him she usually kept by him, and asked him more questions than did any of the other children.

'Yes, Manda, I've seen them feeding their young.'

'Did you climb up to the eyrie?'

'Yes, I did. But it's a long time ago.'

'Was it dangerous?' asked Simon eagerly. 'Can we go up?'

'It isn't particularly dangerous,' Andrew said, adding, 'But it would be difficult for you to get up there. Besides, we don't know where there's an eyrie.'

'Meredith does,' put in Robbie. 'He said he'd been watching one and that there were two eggs and they both hatched but one eaglet died afterwards.'

'Only two eggs?' said Thomas. 'That's not many.'

'Eagles often lay only one,' Andrew told him.

'Why did one die?' Marilyn had been running on a little way in front with Shena, but she stopped to put her question to Andrew.

'It would have been a weakly bird. Did Meredith say how old it was, Robbie?'

'Six weeks—and they're big by then.'

'Ah, well the mother would have been feeding them both and so they'd have shared the food equally, but at six weeks she would just leave the food and expect them to tear it up themselves. If one eaglet was weaker then the other would get all the food.'

'Natural selection,' commented Roger.

'Exactly.'

'What's natural selection?' asked Shena, but this time Andrew just laughed and ruffled her hair.

'You'll know when you're older, Shena,' he replied when she repeated her question. 'Look,' he said suddenly. 'There's an eagle—over against the cliff.'

They all stopped immediately, uttering little gasps of admiration as they watched the graceful aquiline performance of a golden eagle as it dived, wings half open, straight down the cliff; then, coming out of the dive it spread its wings and glided effortlessly across the broad glen, expertly using the air currents until it rose again with a majestic movement of its wings.

'Its eyrie will be on the top of the cliff, won't it, Daddy?'

Andrew nodded.

'Yes, Robbie—see, it's alighting.' It was instantly lost to sight and they all began walking again, along a path above the glen.

'What a size!' exclaimed Harvey. 'I'd hate that to attack me!'

'They don't attack men,' said his wife. 'Do they, Gail?'

She laughed and said she didn't know. Andrew replied for her.

'They could, if you went too near their eyrie—have been known to, in fact, but it's very rare. In any case, it's more of a "frightening off" performance done with their wings. A stalker of mine was attacked in this way once, but the eagle never actually touched him.'

'It it true that they take lambs?'

'Yes, they'll take lambs, and full-grown foxes. Fox cubs are often found outside the eyrie—or the inedible remains of the cubs, I should say.'

'I can imagine them taking the cubs', put in Gail, 'but the full-grown animals.... Don't they fight the eagles?'

'I expect they put up some sort of resistance', he said, looking at her. 'But have you ever seen the talons of an eagle?'

'No, I haven't—and I don't think I want to get close enough to see them, either,' returned Gail with a shudder.

'Daddy doesn't mind if the eagles take the lambs,' remarked Robbie unconcernedly. 'Do you, Daddy?'

'I certainly do mind,' came the swift reply. 'What gave you that idea?'

110

'Because you never shoot the eagles, and neither does Meredith. Not like the foxes—he gets mad with them and goes off to find their dens.'

'We don't shoot the eagles, no. But we don't like them taking the lambs for all that.'

'It seems to me,' interposed Beth a little sadly, 'that everything's out to kill everything else.'

'That's inevitable where you get wild life,' returned Andrew. 'Many animals must kill in order to live themselves and I even feel sorry for the foxes sometimes. They must become desperate when they've several ravenous cubs to feed.' His words were so unexpected that Gail raised her head sharply to look at him. He smiled and his glance seemed to say, 'Yes, Gail, I do have a heart,' and her own smile broke in response because she felt happy and warm and stangely reassured.

CHAPTER SEVEN

THE time sped away quickly and with only two days to go Heather's face became glum as she said, on finding herself alone with Gail,

'I've never enjoyed a holiday so much; I simply hate the thought of going home. Do ask us again soon, won't you?'

Gail nodded and smiled The company had been good for her, but of far greater importance to Gail was the enjoyment Andrew had derived from the rest and the change. Roger was of course an old friend, but Harvey also had much in common with Andrew, and Gail could envisage many more such visits to Dunlochrie House.

On the afternoon prior to the departure of the two families Shena had her birthday party, Andrew having earlier suggested it be brought forward a few days so that her four cousins could attend. The three sisters were doing most of the work themselves, a circumstance that brought a questioning look from Andrew when he heard of it. It was as if he failed to understand their taking on a task that could be done by the kitchen staff.

'It's the sort of thing a mother wants to do herself—a sort of labour of love.' Heather made this remark, for Gail would never have done so, and something suddenly woke in Andrew's eyes as he looked down at his wife's eager face.

'I'm glad I married you,' he whispered, leaning over her.

She started and blushed.

'Andrew, thank you,' she breathed, and through her swept the memory of his lips pressed fleetingly to the scar on her temple. Often she had thought of it, wondering whether it had been an automatic gesture

112

prompted by her distress, and one of which he himself was scarcely aware, or whether he also had recurring recollections of it. If so, the idea of a repetition had not occurred to him—or, more likely, it held no attraction for him. But now he smiled at her in a way that made her excitingly content with the moment, conscious as she was of her sisters' interest in this intimate little interchange of words and looks.

'Are you all coming to the party?' asked Beth of her husband, who had just joined them.

'Well. . . .' he began, and that was as far as he got.

'You are,' Beth told him. 'So don't get any ideas of sidling off somewhere and having quiet drinks all on your own!' Her words included Andrew, to whom she turned, laughing and, glancing up at her husband, Gail was fully prepared to witness that familiar lift of brows followed by a firm if tactful sentence designed to put Beth in her place. But from the first Beth had made a hit with him and to Gail's surprise he only laughed, whereupon Beth added, 'You can also entertain the children while we prepare the room. We don't want them to see it until teatime.'

'Just a minute,' protested Harvey. 'Looking after children isn't man's work!'

Beth's eyes opened wide.

'You helped produce them, so you can just do your share,' she returned in firm decisive tones, and again Andrew laughed.

'We'll take them out and find something to keep them occupied,' he promised obligingly.

'Let's play putting,' Simon eagerly suggested when the time came to discuss what they would do.

'You've been on that green every possible minute,' said his mother. 'It looks as if we're to have a famous golfer in the family.'

'I'd like to play cricket for a change,' said Manda.

'We'll be quite a long while, so you'll have time for both—and a swim for that matter.'

The big dining-room was used, for in addition to the

six, over twenty of Shena's and Robbie's friends had been invited, and Gail and her sisters worked until lunchtime, decorating the room with streamers and balloons, with fairy lights and masses of flowers. The table would be set immediately after lunch; the three men were to sit with the children while their wives did the waiting on.

At lunch time Robbie and Shena came into the house first, followed by their father.

'We'll go and wash our hands and faces,' said Robbie, and they both ran off to one of the cloakrooms at the end of the hall.

'If that had been my two they'd have wanted to see the room—even though they would expect to be refused.' Heather frowned, sending a puzzled glance from Andrew to Gail.

Andrew said, a faintly bitter edge to his voice,

'They're not used to having the room decorated. This is the first time it's been done.'

'The first——?' Heather pulled herself up, realizing her lack of tact. 'Then it'll be a nice surprise for them.'

'It will indeed,' and his glance of gratitude was divided between all three girls as he looked at them in turn.

And it was a surprise. Other birthday parties, arranged by indifferent nannies with no desire for extra work, had merely meant a table full of dry ham sandwiches and cake and whatever the kitchen staff had been ordered to produce. But all three sisters were fully experienced in preparing a children's party, with Gail herself particularly active when such things were going on.

And because of their experience the table glittered even as the room did. The sandwiches, filled with chopped meats and chicken, were cut into shapes and then burnt slightly on a grid which gave them curls and stripes and all sorts of other decorations. The small cakes were colourfully decorated with care and

114

imagination, the biscuits took on animals shapes. Jellies scintillated in the light; there was a huge trifle and of course the birthday cake with Shena's name and six red candles ready to be lit.

While the girls had been occupied with the table the men were busy with the ever-increasing family on the lawn outside, devising games and competitions with prizes for the winners—and in fact for every single child.

'I suggest,' said Heather, 'that as Shena and Robbie haven't had a similar treat before, they should come in first so they can take a good look at the room on their own.'

'That's a good idea,' agreed Beth. 'I'll go and fetch them. But when she returned Andrew was also with her. He stood by the door; Gail looked at him and thought she saw a strange emotional movement in his throat.

'Mummy!' breathed Shena, her small hands clasped tightly against her. 'Oh, what have you done! I've never had a party like this before. It's beautiful!' She and her brother just looked round in rapturous wonderment for a while before Shena spoke to Andrew. 'Daddy, isn't it wonderful?'

'It is, Shena.' He seemed unable to articulate further words for a moment, but eventually he looked down affectionately at his daughter and told her to thank her aunties and her mummy for all the trouble they had taken. This she did at once; they smiled at her and then Heather nudged Gail, drawing her attention to Robbie, standing there, still wide-eyed, but with his mouth now obviously watering as his gaze was directed at the table.

'Will it be like this at my party?' he asked on becoming aware of the amused stares of all four adults.

'Of course, Robbie,' answered Gail, and her husband added,

'We shall have to ask your aunties to come and help, shan't we? Robbie's birthday is on Christmas Eve,' he informed Beth and Heather. His words were clearly an invitation and, judging by their expressions, they were readily accepting the invitation. Gail looked away, a tightness in her throat. This was more than she could take in all at once and she was a little afraid of disgracing herself by allowing the tears to escape.

'Shall I let the others come in?' Andrew asked, and Heather nodded.

'Yes, we're quite ready for them.' And she added ruefully, 'You're sitting with them, and the din will be awful. Do you mind?'

'I shall thoroughly enjoy it,' he replied, and meant it.

Bedlam reigned for the next hour or two and then parents began appearing to take their children home.

Shena was put to bed, tired but happy. After Gail had tucked her in she sat up, throwing her arms round Gail's neck and hugging her.

'I love you—my mummy,' she said, kissing her. 'I love you very much. Thank you for my beautiful party!'

'And I love you, my pet,' responded Gail huskily, ignoring Shena's last sentence. 'Goodnight, darling.'

Her eyes were bright when she joined the others downstairs. They were in the sitting-room and both her sisters were on the couch, exhausted.

'I always say I'll never have another party,' laughed Heather, gratefully taking the glass handed to her by Andrew. 'I'm absolutely drained!'

'No wonder; you've all worked like Trojans.' Andrew's eyes thanked her as he added, 'Shena will remember this party all her life.'

'You men did your part,' admitted Beth with mock reluctance. 'I expect the success was a result of teamwork.'

'Thank you,' said her husband acidly. 'I was beginning to wonder when our contribution would be recognized!'

They went early the following morning, Andrew having invited them to come again in a few weeks for the grouse shooting. Harvey had reluctantly to decline, not only because he would be working, but also because he was not a very good shot. Roger, being his own boss, willingly accepted, his children plainly delighted when their father said they could have a few days off school so that they and their mother could come with him.

'You'll all come for Christmas?' Andrew said, noting the rather crestfallen faces of the other two children.

Harvey nodded.

'We'd love to, Andrew, and thank you for inviting us.'

They all piled into the two cars and soon they were driving away, with Gail and Andrew, and the two children, standing on the forecourt, waving until the cars were lost to view down the mile-long avenue leading to the main road.

'I wonder why Mrs. Davis didn't come,' remarked Gail later when she and Andrew were chatting after lunch.

'I rang and asked her not to,' he returned abruptly, clearly leaving much unsaid. But Gail knew he hadn't wanted anything to mar the holiday, and the presence of his mother-in-law would certainly have put a temporary damper on everyone's spirits.

She looked at him, and with her deep understanding of how he felt she admired him for allowing his late wife's mother to visit her grandchildren when clearly her presence was an annoyance to him, for it was obvious that he did not like her. He would do his duty, whatever the cost, she decided, and wondered again if it had been merely a sense of duty which impelled him to take his wife back, forgiving her indiscretions.

Everything fell a little flat after the visitors had gone, with Andrew resuming his work and Robbie and Shena seeming rather lost after having had four boisterous cousins for company.

'We've nothing to do,' sighed Robbie. 'I wish they could have stayed longer.'

'Can't we go on a picnic?' suggested Shena, hopefully looking up at Gail.

'Tomorrow, darling——'

'Why not today?'

'Because your grandmother's coming to see you. She telephoned me this morning to tell me.' To her dismay both children pouted and she added quickly, 'You like your grandmother to come and see you, I'm sure—and you must remember to be nice to her and show your pleasure at her visit.'

'Pleasure!' scoffed Robbie, kicking at the corner of the hearthrug. 'I don't like her!'

'Neither do I.' Shena's eyes suddenly sparkled. 'If you take us on a picnic we won't see her.'

Gail tilted her head admonishingly.

'I've just said, Shena, that your grandmother rang this morning to tell me she was coming. It would be very bad manners to be out, now wouldn't it?'

'Do you like her coming??' asked Robbie, looking at Gail with a strangely perceptive expression in his blue eyes.

'She comes to see you, not me,' was the instant rejoinder before Gail diplomatically changed the subject. 'If it's fine tomorrow we'll take the car and go for a long ride, then have our lunch in the woods. How will that suit you?'

Both children brightened at that, but an hour later when Mrs. Davis drove up the pouts appeared again.

'I'm taking them home for tea,' said their grandmother, refusing Gail's offer of refreshment. 'My husband wants to see them.'

'I don't want——'

'Run and wash your face and hands,' interrupted Gail hastily. 'Shena, come along, I'll help you. Robbie, do as you're told!'

'Do we have to go, Mummy?' wailed Shena as the sponge was applied to her face.

'Certainly you must go.' Gail's voice was firm, but inwardly she felt it was wrong to force the children into going with their grandmother. True, their grandfather would derive pleasure from their visit, but the children themselves would be miserable. It was not as if they were old enough to understand the position, or to realize that they must on occasions make sacrifices for the pleasure of others.

'You're too possessive with them,' snapped Mrs. Davis when on their return to her, washed and changed, she saw their glum faces. 'I must speak to Andrew. They never used to be like this.'

'It's nothing,' said Gail, anxious to smooth it over. 'They've had company for a fortnight and now they're feeling a little lost.'

'Your sisters' children, I believe.' The woman gave her a flickering glance of contempt. 'Was Andrew ashamed of his in-laws? Was that why he asked me to keep away?'

Gail's eyes sparkled.

'Andrew doesn't consider himself superior to my family, Mrs. Davis!'

'Then he must have changed,' came the swift retort. 'He's always considered himself superior to everybody!'

'I'm not inclined to discuss either my husband or my family with you,' Gail told her icily. 'The children are ready whenever you are.'

She watched them go, her blood boiling when at last she turned away from the window. She had meant to keep calm, ignoring the woman's insolent comments, but the more she thought of them the higher rose her temper. And it was unfortunate, to say the least, that Morag should happen to arrive at that particular time. She was in a car driven by a dowdy young man who, having watched Morag take her luggage from the car unaided, made a wide sweep on the forecourt and roared off down the drive.

Gail watched the girl walk unsteadily into the house,

carrying a suitcase and a smaller piece of hand luggage.

Was Morag drunk? A frown appeared on Gail's face, and she turned as the girl entered the room, having left her luggage in the hall.

'Hello,' laughed Morag a trifle hysterically. 'Where is everyone? Get me a drink, will you?'

'*I* get you a drink?' snapped Gail. 'It seems to me you've had enough already! And since when have you expected me to wait upon you?'

The girl moved unsteadily to a chair.

'My, but you're in a temper. Had a row with your husband, Mrs. MacNeill?' She put a hand to her head and Gail moved from the window, further into the room, utter disgust in her eyes.

'Don't you think you'd better have some black coffee?' she suggested in icy tones. 'Shall I ring for some?'

'Black coffee—ugh! No, Mrs. MacNeill, it's brandy I want—a stiff one!'

'You won't get brandy while I'm here!'

'Then for God's sake take yourself off, because it's brandy I need!' She tried to rise, her eyes on the bottle standing on the sideboard. Wrathfully Gail pushed her back in the chair.

'You'll have coffee or nothing!' and Gail picked up the brandy bottle and put it in the cupboard, locking the door and slipping the key into her pocket. 'Now, the best thing you can do is to go to bed and sleep it off——' She stopped, flushing as her husband came and stood in the open doorway. This was not her business, and she would never have interfered had she not been in such a temper over the comments made by Mrs. Davis about her family.

'What's wrong?' Andrew advanced into the room, his eyes on Morag, their expression, much to Gail's surprise, portraying anxiety rather than anger. 'Morag, are you ill?'

Ill. . . . Gail's heart turned right over. Had she misjudged the girl?

'I'm not exactly in the pink of condition,' replied Morag, glaring balefully at her stepmother. '*She* won't give me the brandy!'

'Is she ill?' asked Gail fearfully, noticing that Morag now had a hand to her heart. 'I didn't know—I thought——'

'Where is the brandy?' he demanded, glancing at the sideboard. Gail took the key from her pocket, aware of his sudden anger.

'I'm sorry ... I thought it was for the best. Shall I pour some out for her?'

He was standing over Morag, his hand on her wrist. 'Yes—but not much. Then phone for the doctor.'

Gail handed him the glass, colouring under his gaze.

'Is it serious?' she faltered, contrition flooding over her. Why had she been so ready to condemn?—but she would not have done so had she not been in such a fury. Unreasonably Gail blamed Mrs. Davis for what had happened. 'Would—would it have made any difference if I'd given her the brandy right away?'

Aware of her deep anxiety, he shook his head, although a trifle impatiently.

'Don't let it trouble you.' He was holding the glass to Morag's pallid lips; she seemed scarcely capable of swallowing, and suddenly began to cough. 'I asked you to phone the doctor.'

'Yes.' Gail sped away, her heart beating wildly. Andrew's face was so set and grave. Was Morag seriously ill?

'What happened?' inquired Andrew some time later after the doctor had been and Morag was in bed. 'Why did you put the brandy away?'

'I thought—thought she'd had——' Gail broke off, embarrassed, and her husband finished for her,

'—she'd had too much already, eh? Well, that's understandable, I suppose.'

'I feel awful. There really was no excuse. I should have made sure.' Her face was pale and anxious. 'Do you think it's as serious as the doctor says?'

'I don't think he'd exaggerate. Morag certainly has a heart disease and as he says, if the tablets don't prove effective she'll have to have an operation.'

Gail nodded, her eyes downcast. She felt overwhelmed with guilt at not having seen at once that Morag was ill.

'I feel awful,' she said again in some distress. 'I wasn't nice to Morag when she came in—in fact, I was so cross with her that I actually pushed her into the chair—— Oh, Andrew, do you think that would have done her any harm?'

They were standing by the window, where they could see the children playing on the swings, and Andrew turned to Gail, his grave set face breaking into a smile, a difficult smile, but one produced for the sole purpose of reassuring her.

'Gail dear,' he said softly, 'you mustn't blame yourself for anything.' And before she could speak he had placed a finger under her chin, lifting her face to his. Gently he kissed her lips, his smile returning and deepening as on drawing away he watched the colour begin to fluctuate in her cheeks and a starry light momentarily enter her eyes before they shadowed again as her thoughts returned to Morag.

'We must be very kind to her, Andrew,' she murmured, and he nodded firmly.

'Yes, Gail, we must be very kind to her.'

But despite her good resolutions Gail had the greatest difficulty in being kind to Morag, for even in her illness she was totally unresponsive and often there came back to Gail the words her husband had uttered about Morag's not being capable of feeling hurt because she was invulnerable to pain. She seemed to float in a vacuum of immunity to any form of emotion, staring always into space and ignoring any efforts at approach which Gail might make.

After a fortnight in bed she was allowed to get up. Andrew and Gail were relieved that the tablets were proving effective. But of course she must take care, the doctor had said, and it would seem her escapades were at an end, much to everyone's satisfaction except that of Morag herself who would sit and sulk and repeatedly declare life was not worth living. Her grandmother had been anxious and she too was obviously glad that Morag would not be running off again, leaving everyone wondering where she was.

The young man who brought her home had not even telephoned and when Andrew tactfully inquired about him Morag said he wasn't anyone important—just one of her boy-friends.

'Of all the friends she's supposed to have had, not one has inquired about her,' murmured Andrew sadly, adding, 'It's to be hoped she now knows their true worth.'

Robin asked about her, however, one day when he came to fish in the loch.

'Would you like to come in and speak to her?' invited Gail eagerly, thinking Morag would welcome a young man visitor.

'I don't know,' began Robin doubtfully. 'With all due respect, Gail, she isn't my type.'

'Does that matter? She's confined to the house, and it's dull for her. Do come and talk to her, Robin.'

'All right,' he agreed at length. 'I'll stay and have a chat with her.'

Gail introduced them ... and little did she know what the repercussions of her action were going to be. For Morag had not changed and when Robin had gone she said to Gail, in the old sneering and insolent way,

'What's the game? Don't get any ideas that you can use me to further your own ends. Robin's your boy-friend, not mine, and I'll take good care Father's not deceived.'

Shocked, Gail could only stare for a while, unwilling to believe what she heard.

'Morag, how can you! I brought Robin in here in all good faith, believing his company would be a nice break for you. I'm not in the least interested in Robin, nor he in me.'

'How well you do it!' Morag's sharp eyes gleamed with an almost evil light. 'It won't work, Mrs. Mac-Neill. How you came to put Father off the last time I don't know, because he was furious when I told him about you and Robin. But you won't get round him again; he's had too much experience. My mother was like you—unfaithful!' Sick with disgust and disappointment, Gail had nothing to say and Morag continued, amused by her expression, 'One has only to watch the way Robin looks at you to know what's going on.'

'The way——?' She stopped and a faint flush mounted her cheeks as she recalled Robin's saying it was just his luck that she was married—but at the time she had laughed, thinking nothing of it. Later, when he wanted to fish, she had experienced that strange uneasiness. And then had occurred that scene when Andrew furiously forbade her to speak to Robin again. The raising of his suspicions had all been Morag's doing, but her efforts to bring about a lasting rift had failed utterly—they had in fact brought Gail and her husband close together, a circumstance which must have puzzled Morag exceedingly. 'You're imagining things,' she said, but feebly.

Morag laughed, and leant back on the couch, her head coming to rest against the cushions.

'Frightened? You'll be more than frightened when Father's suspicions become really aroused. You've never seen the side of him that I have—but you will if you don't take care. If you really knew him you'd not have your boy-friend coming to the house—— After all, you've plenty of opportunity of seeing him outside, when Robbie and Shena are at school. I would, in your position.'

'You haven't changed a bit, have you?' said Gail disgustedly.

'Changed? Why should I change?'

124

'I thought your illness would have made you see sense—would have made you realize how harmful that sort of life was.'

'What sort of a life?' queried Morag interestedly.

'You used to boast that you could stay up all night, that you did in fact do so at these various parties you attended. And you drink and smoke too much. These things are harmful and that's why you're ill.'

'I'm not ill; I'm better.'

'You still have to take care. You're not better, Morag, you know that.'

The younger girl's mouth tightened.

'I am better! And what's more I'm going away again soon. I rang up a friend yesterday and he wants me to join him and some others who are going on holiday.'

Startled, Gail asked if Morag had informed her father of this, and when Morag shook her head Gail spoke quickly, before the other girl could do so.

'Then I shall enlighten him; it would be harmful if you were to go against the doctor's orders, and those orders are that you have complete rest.'

A threatening gleam entered Morag's eyes. Raising her head from the cushions, she leant forward.

'You'll tell him to your cost!'

Gail frowned.

'What do you mean by that, may I ask?'

'I mean,' returned Morag slowly and deliberately, 'that I also can do some enlightening—about you and Robin. Tell Father I'm going away and I shall tell him you brought Robin in today!'

Pale, but determined, Gail reasserted her intention of warning Andrew of Morag's intentions.

'I shall tell him why I brought Robin in, and he'll believe me,' she ended, wondering at the sudden dryness in her mouth.

'What you tell him, and what he thinks, will not, I'm afraid, coincide. Father suspects every woman of deceit—and no one can really blame him,' she added with a laugh. 'First Mother, and then me——' She laughed again, quite unashamedly, and Gail turned away. There were times when she could not bear to see the evil expression on this girl's face.

What should she do? she asked herself over and over again during the next few hours while Andrew was still out. His fury over Robin had been quite out of proportion, because he had nothing concrete on which to base that fury. Life had been so pleasant recently and her hopes for the future had soared. In ordinary circumstances her husband would have trusted her and it would have taken much more than a little malicious tale-carrying on Morag's part to arouse his suspicions about Gail . . . but with his past experience of his late wife's infidelity, and his present abiding anxiety over Morag. . . .

Never had Gail been so undecided. Strong of character and unhesitating in her decisions where her duty was concerned, she had never before been in such a quandary.

It was a long while before she made up her mind, but she did at last reach a decision. For she would carry the weight of blame for the rest of her life if anything happened to Morag when she, Gail, was in a position to prevent it.

CHAPTER EIGHT

On receiving Gail's information Andrew strode off immediately, anger portrayed in his every step. The sitting-room door was flung open, then closed with more noise than was usually associated with Andrew's movements. Gail went up to the nursery, busying herself with tidying up the children's toys and books and waiting with a wildly beating heart for her husband's reaction to Morag's false and malicious insinuations about Robin and herself. Surely he would see that these were born of frustration and revenge, thought Gail, even while she was recalling that other frightening scene, and trembling a little as she relived it.

She heard his footsteps taking the stairs two at a time and wondered if he had been searching for her downstairs, and whether that had increased his anger ... *if* he were angry.

If. . . .

His jaw was tight, his blue eyes dark and hard as steel as he walked into the nursery and stood there, regarding her in silence for a space before he snapped,

'Is it true that you had Robin in the house today?'

'Yes, Andrew,' she returned quietly, holding one of Robbie's books against her in a little protective gesture, as if it were a shield against the onslaught that was to come. 'I thought he would be company for Morag.'

His lips twisted; the movement filled her with a sense of his injustice even before he spoke.

'Company for Morag? You expect me to believe that?'

Gail tried to excuse him, thinking of his late wife's infidelity, but her anger rose above her understanding.

'Just what are you accusing me of, Andrew?'

'I told you not to speak to the man again!'

She looked squarely at him.

'It's not like you to be evasive; I asked you a question. In any case, I thought we'd settled the matter of my not speaking to Robin again. You still allow him to come to the loch.' Her eyes were sparkling, the only sign as yet of her rising temper.

He still evaded her question.

'I'd like to know the real reason for his visit.'

'I've told you, I thought he would be company for Morag.' It was in the nursery that the other scene had occurred, she suddenly recalled, and wished she had remained downstairs. The nursery was an attractive, intimate place to her, with the children's things all about. Anger and dissension seemed out of place in such an atmosphere.

'The last time,' he said in grating tones, 'you gave the children as your excuse—said they wanted to walk with this man——'

'I've no need to make excuses,' she broke in quiveringly. 'One only makes excuses when one has something to hide!'

'And haven't you anything to hide?'

'Nothing!' she flashed. 'How dare you speak to me like this? How dare you put me on the same level as—as——?' She stopped, unable even in her anger to throw his dead wife's failing in his face. 'I should have thought you'd have sufficient understanding of Morag's character to know that her insinuations were prompted by malice,' she went on in more controlled tones.

He had gone a trifle pale, and it struck her that it came as a complete surprise to him to learn that she had heard stories about his late wife. On the last occasion similar to this, she recalled, he had said he had an excuse for his suspicions, but had refused to elaborate on that excuse, unwilling, naturally, to talk about the past and its unpleasant memories.

'What reason have you for suggesting that Morag should feel malicious towards you?' he asked, more quietly now, but continuing to regard her with hardness and suspicion in his eyes.

'You're not obtuse!' she retorted, and as his eyes glinted dangerously she suspected he would shake her again if she continued to speak to him in this vein.

'Take care,' he advised. 'I warned you once before, remember?' Prudently she fell silent, turning aside to place the book on Robbie's little desk. 'About this man,' he said, reverting to the question of Robin. 'He doesn't come here again. Is that clear?'

Gail faced him again.

'If you say he can't come, then he can't.' A small pause as Gail saw the little start he gave, as if taken aback at her acceptance of his authority. 'I asked you what you're accusing me of,' she then said, watching him closely. His anger had diminished quite suddenly, but his mouth retained its stiff uncompromising line.

'At present, nothing, but I'm making sure I'll never again be made a fool of—oh, yes, you obviously know about my previous experiences, so there's no longer any need for silence on my part. This time, my wife will behave with the decorum her position demands. I'll not have men calling here in my absence; get that firmly fixed in your head, otherwise your life will be damned unpleasant.' And with that dark warning he left her, drained and unhappy, as she was on that other occasion.

But on that other occasion he has softened, their quarrel ending in a gentle kiss that had taken her by breathless surprise and sent her hopes for the future soaring heavenwards.

She sat down when he had gone and tears filled her eyes. Why had she saved Morag at this cost to herself? Silence would have been the safer course. But Gail had followed the dictates of her conscience, gambling on Andrew's trusting her—and she had lost. Nevertheless, even in her misery she knew she would do the same again, for Morag must be saved from her own reck-lessness.

The children were at dancing class; with a little start Gail realized the time, and rushed downstairs.

'I was just sending for you,' snapped Andrew, unsoftened by the evidence of tears. 'You're going to be late for the children!'

At the sting in his voice her lips quivered, but she went silently past him and out to the car. For the first time she was oblivious of the beauty around her—the tree-lined drive and heather moors, and the mountains drenched in sunlight, as she dwelt on the scene just enacted. In her need to fill the void in her life brought about by the accident, in her desperation to have children in her care and to know the love of those children, she had snatched eagerly at marriage with Andrew, accepting with a kind of humble gratitude the position of wife in name only ... but little had she known that her life must be lived under the shadow of suspicion and distrust resulting from the indiscretions of his former wife.

Gail thought about his reminding her of his previous warning; he had remembered only the quarrel itself, apparently, and not the ending when he had seen her scar and had suddenly become gentle and contrite, taking her in his arms and kissing her. The fact that he could have forgotten what was to her so vivid and important a memory, swelling her heart with hope, brought the tears to her eyes again. To Andrew it meant nothing, while to Gail it had been a promise of a glorious tomorrow, the first seed of affection that would gradually grow into love.

So much for her optimism. Love was not for her. She accepted this now, wondering that she should ever have reached so high. Morag had firmly asserted that he still cherished his dead wife's memory, but Gail could not accept this, for there had been little or no happiness in his marriage. No, it was not love she had to combat, but suspicion and distrust and a deep-rooted bitterness which by its spreading growth was in itself protective.

Andrew would never again be exposed to hurt.

'Mummy,' exclaimed Shena excitedly on getting into the car a short while later, 'how long is it till Simon and Manda come?'

'Only three days. It will soon go.'

'I'll be glad when they come. Will they stay long?'

'They'll stay with us at least a week, I suppose.'

'That's a long time! Oh, I wish they were coming tomorrow, though, because I can hardly wait!'

Robbie came more slowly; he stared at Gail and said with a hint of anxiety unusual in so young a child,

'Have you been crying, Mummy?'

'Crying? Of course——' She stopped before her denial was voiced, unwilling to lie to him. 'I had a little pain, Robbie.'

'A pain? Is it better now?' He was in the car and she felt his cheek against hers as he leant over her seat. 'I don't like you having a pain.'

'Yes, darling, it's better now.'

She took it for granted he would forget all about it, but as soon as he entered the house he said to Andrew,

'Mummy was crying because she had a pain!' Andrew merely cast her an indifferent glance and Robbie added frowningly, 'Don't you care about Mummy's pain?'

'I said it was better,' put in Gail with haste.

'Yes—but it must have hurt, because you wouldn't cry if it didn't. Daddy——'

'Mummy says the pain's better, Robbie, so let the matter drop!'

The child stared in disbelief at the sharpness of his father's words, and his lip quivered. After throwing Gail a glowering look Andrew went out, and for the first time in weeks she and the children took their tea on their own.

Morag was naturally furious with Gail. Her father had taken all her money from her, and had also told Mrs. Birchan to see that a watch was kept on her during the day. At night one of the maids was to sleep in her room.

'And if you get up to any of your tantrums you'll have another attack and be taken straight to hospital,' he had warned Morag.

'It's all your doing!' she told Gail, her eyes blazing. 'You're a spiteful pig—and I hate you!'

'I acted for your own good.' Gail spoke quietly because she feared the consequences should the girl become over-excited. 'You need plenty of rest and you wouldn't get that if you went to stay with your friends.'

'I got my own back, though!'

Gail inclined her head.

'Yes, Morag, you did.'

'I warned you I'd tell Father the truth about you and Robin——'

'They were lies, Morag, mischievous lies.'

'They weren't! So you needn't put on that air of injured innocence. Was Father mad? He was in a white-hot fury when he left me.'

Gail heaved a deep sigh. Nothing would have afforded her greater satisfaction than to tear into this girl, but she dared not create a situation that would arouse Morag's emotions.

'If it's any satisfaction to you, your lies have caused an unnecessary rift between us. Have you no conscience? Don't you ever feel ashamed of yourself?'

'Never,' laughed Morag carelessly. 'As for a conscience—that must be a very uncomfortable thing to possess and I'm sure I'm far happier without one.' She paused, eyeing Gail in faint amusement. 'So Father's really angry with you this time—and how doleful you look! I'm glad he's seen through you at last, though. He was becoming quite soft in his old age.'

'He was becoming a little happier than he had been,' Gail correctedly quietly. 'And now you've spoiled it all.'

'Happier? You give yourself credit for that?'

'I didn't say so.'

'You implied it. What an opinion you have of yourself! Let me tell you this, Mrs. MacNeill, you'll never be anything more than the nanny you are now. Had Father been thinking of a happy marriage he'd have looked for someone he could love, not merely taken on someone to look after the children.' Morag leant back against the cushions and stared at Gail for a long moment, her lips twisted in a sneer. 'Can't you see you're wasting your time? He'll never fall for you, so you might just as well give up.'

It occurred to Gail that Morag was inconsistent in her statements, one moment implying that Gail was far too friendly with Robin, and the next moment that she cherished hopes of finding happiness with her husband. But as Gail had neither the patience nor the inclination to point this out she allowed the matter to rest, saying instead that it was time for Morag to take her tablets.

'I'll get you a drink,' she ended, rising from her chair and at the same time wondering why she took the trouble of making time to sit with Morag each day. It was always an uncomfortable interlude for Gail and she felt half inclined to leave the girl to her own devices in future.

But these thoughts fled as, on her return, she saw Morag lying back on the couch, her lips blue and her breathing laboured.

'Are you ill again?' she asked fearfully, wondering where Andrew was. He had been around only half an hour ago. 'Come,' she said gently, easing Morag's head up. 'Take your tablets.' Morag swallowed them and after a short while she seemed better. 'Have you some pain?'

'Don't be an idiot! Of course I've some pain!'

'I'll get Mrs. Birchan and we'll put you to bed——'

'I'm not going to bed. I had a fortnight of that and it was quite enough to last me for a long time.'

'What's wrong?' Andrew stood in the doorway, frowning. 'Has she had another attack?' he inquired of Gail and, when she nodded, 'Was it bad?'

'Of course it wasn't bad,' snapped Morag. 'She wants to be rid of me, though, but I'm not going to bed.'

'We'll see about that,' said Andrew crisply. 'Gail, fetch Mrs. Birchan.'

Protesting, but helpless, Morag was put to bed by the two women while Andrew telephoned for the doctor.

'Keep her in bed,' ordered the doctor. 'I'll give her another couple of weeks on the tablets, and then we'll see what's to be done.' He was with Andrew in the hall; Gail heard them talking as she came downstairs, having left the housekeeper with Morag.

'Wouldn't it be better if she had the operation at once?' Andrew asked anxiously.

The doctor looked straight at him.

'We're old friends, Andrew,' he said, 'and so you won't take offence at what I'm about to say. The life Morag's lived has undermined her constitution—and an operation would be touch and go.'

'I see. . . .' Andrew's face was taut and grim. He turned abstractedly to glance at Gail as she reached the bottom of the stairs. Her heart went out to him and she yearned to give him comfort, but he followed the doctor to the door, in the same abstracted way, and Gail went along to the kitchen to prepare the children's tea.

The breach between them remained, but Andrew was obliged to effect a superficial friendliness towards his wife during the time of the shooting party which, after some indecision, he decided not to postpone, for there was nothing to be gained. Morag had a nurse with her during the day and the maid still slept in her room at night. This was in deference to Morag's own wish; she did not want a stranger sleeping in her room, she had told Andrew.

The weather being fine and warm, the men were out each day—Andrew and Roger and several other friends whom he had invited for the shoot. They would talk about it over dinner, mentioning their bags, and

Gail would look at them in turn and wonder how they could derive such pleasure from the slaughter of defenceless birds. Foxes were an altogether different matter; their need causing them to kill the lambs, but as far as Gail could see the grouse never harmed anything.

'Gail hates this sport,' commented Andrew one evening on noticing her lack of appetite and putting it down to the conversation. 'Perhaps we should change the subject.'

She glanced gratefully at him, but already he had looked away, and she was left in doubt as to whether his words were spoken merely for effect or, as she optimistically hoped, in consideration for her feelings.

The following day, Ian, one of the guests, gave her the comforting information that one of the drives had been ruined by the circling of an eagle over the area. The beaters had fanned out and were sending the grouse to the butts when the appearance of the eagle created panic among them. At the beginning of the season the grouse were not normally off the ground, but the presence of this enemy resulted in a mass flight of the grouse who, with a tail wind to aid them, soon disappeared at a speed of about eighty miles an hour.

'I'm glad they escaped,' declared Gail with satisfaction, uncaring as to whether or not anyone was amused by her words. 'I don't know how you can be so heartless.'

Andrew drew an exasperated breath.

'I've explained that the numbers must be kept down in order to maintain food supplies,' he reminded her shortly. 'Also, with high densities of game disease could soon become rampant.'

'Another thing,' put in Roger, supporting his friend, 'we don't have loaders, if that's any comfort to you.'

'What difference does that make?' demanded Heather, no happier than her sister about this sport.

'We fire two shots and then have to do our own reloading. That means the birds do have a sporting chance.'

'How very kind and humane,' was his wife's sarcastic retort. 'I'm afraid, Roger, your efforts at vindication are far too weak to be effective.' Her eyes met those of her brother-in-law; in his there was a sort of bored contempt, in hers a challenge.

'Shall we go into the lounge?' invited Gail hastily. 'The coffee will be ready.'

'He hasn't changed a bit!' The exclamation of disgust came from Heather as she and Gail sat together on the couch in the lounge, their coffee on a small table in front of them. The men were engrossed in the subject of sport, and the two girls might not have been there for all the attention they received. 'I thought he had, when I was here before, because he was so nice to you—and to Beth and me for that matter, but this time——' She shooked her head. 'He doesn't like women, Gail. How do you get on with him? If he were my husband I'm sure I should hit him!'

Gail had to laugh.

'You'd be sorry!'

'Indeed?' Heather turned her head and subjected Gail to a rather searching stare. 'You've already had your differences of opinion?'

'I wouldn't describe it quite like that,' answered Gail ruefully, and, on noticing her sister's inquiring, persuasive expression she went on to relate what had occurred as a result of her innocent acquaintanceship with Robin.

'I can't altogether blame Andrew,' she continued after a pause. 'He's suffered, Heather, and his pride's been abominably hurt. And he now seems to be tormented by the idea that were I seen even speaking to another man the wrong conclusions would be drawn—that people would begin to pity him. I was angry, and defiant, but I'm sorry now because I should have been more understanding. Had I reasoned, instead of losing my temper, I'm sure he'd have adopted a more tolerant attitude.'

'Had you allowed yourself to be intimidated, you mean, don't you?' was the swift and scathing rejoinder.

Gail shook her head, becoming thoughtfully silent for a while. On that first occasion Andrew's swift dark fury had melted on his perceiving the scar, melted so suddenly that it could not have been the hard inflexible thing it had appeared when on impulse he had shaken her with such force that she had started to cry. No such providential occurrence had brought a similar happy ending to the second scene, but Gail now had the sure conviction that had she been more conciliatory, reasoning with him in a calm unruffled way, his anger would again have subsided, leaving in its place the tolerance and friendliness she had begun to take for granted. Instead, there now existed this coldness on his part, creating a rift that could soon widen and deepen until it became an insurmountable barrier between them.

'It wasn't intimidation, exactly,' said Gail on suddenly noting her sister's attitude of waiting. 'Andrew was anxious to avoid gossip and that's why he told me I mustn't speak to Robin again. I just flared up, and so he naturally became more angry and——' She broke off, shrugging unhappily. 'We're not very friendly now, as a result of it.'

'He's not been noticeably unfriendly towards you since our coming,' reflected Heather, sending him a glance. 'But there is a difference in his way with you— although I expect he thinks he's successfully hiding it,' she added as an afterthought. Gail said nothing and Heather went on hesitatingly, 'You're still in love with him?'

Gail gave a startled little laugh.

'You don't expect I've fallen *out* of love with him?'

'You're crazy, Gail,' her sister murmured softly. 'If only you'd waited!'

'Waited? What for?'

'Someone really nice to turn up. He would have done, you know—sooner or later.'

'And what about Robbie and Shena? What would have happened to them?' Heather made no answer, but it was not difficult to read her thoughts. They would have had someone else.... Gail frowned darkly at the idea of that. 'They need me, Heather ... and I need them. This is fate—theirs and mine, and if I'd my time to come over again I'd still marry Andrew.' He was looking straight at her and she blushed. His eyes narrowed and his mouth went tight. He knew he was the object of their conversation, and was angry in consequence.

'If you must discuss me,' he said icily when, just as she was going up to bed he stopped her in the hall, 'then please have the manners to do so in my absence!'

The hurt was almost physical. Her lovely eyes held deep reproach as she said,

'If you knew what I was saying, Andrew, then perhaps you wouldn't speak so unkindly to me.' And although she knew he gave an involuntary little start she left him no time to comment as she went past him and mounted the stairs.

The four children could scarcely contain themselves as they waited for Gail and Heather to prepare the food and drinks for the picnic.

'When are we going?' Simon asked impatiently. 'We don't want all that food.'

Heather, cutting sandwiches at the kitchen table, gave him a determined little shove.

'Out! Or you won't come at all!'

'Heather,' began Gail remonstratingly, 'it's only natural they're impatient.'

'You're too soft with them——' She stopped to wave a warning hand towards the children, now clustered by the door. 'I said out—all of you!' They went, heads down, and Gail had to smile. This sort of treatment was entirely new to Shena and Robbie—at least, since the arrival of their stepmother on the scene. 'Wait till you've had them a little while longer; you'll not allow them to tantalize you as they do now.'

'Can you manage?' asked Gail a few minutes later. 'I just want to go up to Morag for a while.'

'Yes, I can manage. How many flasks are we taking?'

'Two. I've made lemonade for the children.'

Morag was sitting up in bed, a sulky expression on her face. The nurse was in a chair, reading the newspaper. Gail nodded and smiled as she passed her and sat down on the bed.

'How do you feel today? You're looking much better.'

'I am much better.' Morag scowled at the nurse as she added irascibly, 'I want to get up!'

The nurse merely raised her head, then resumed her reading.

'The doctor said a fortnight,' Gail gently reminded Morag. 'It's for your own good. You must have complete rest.'

'I know what's for my own good! Where's Father?'

'He'll be up soon.'

Morag crushed the bed cover between her hands.

'He won't let me get up—— Oh, I could scream!'

Gail sighed.

'Why don't you read?' she suggested. 'Shall I look out some books for you and bring them up?'

The girl's eyes swept contemptuously over her.

'The sort of books you'd choose wouldn't be very entertaining. No, I don't want to read in any case.' She paused a moment. 'I want a cigarette,' she then added softly. 'I could smoke it when she goes down for her coffee.'

But Gail shook her head.

'Sorry, Morag, nothing doing. The doctor said definitely no cigarettes.'

'Are you refusing out of concern for me?—or because you're afraid of what Father would say?' Gail had no patience to reply to that and Morag changed the subject, asking Gail where they were all going. 'Your sister said last night that you'd arranged to take the children on a picnic,' she added.

'We haven't decided. I expect we'll decide once we're on the road.'

'What a way to spend your time! I'd be bored to tears with four children around me.'

Gail rose, cutting short her intended stay, and becoming overwhelmed with guilt the moment she had closed the door behind her.

'I feel so mean and selfish,' she told Heather on returning to the kitchen. 'I wish I could have more patience with Morag.'

'Patience—with that one?' Heather picked up the jug of lemonade and began pouring the contents into a bottle. 'I think you're an angel to bother with her at all. I've been up there only twice—and I wanted to leave before the wretched girl had spoken half a dozen words. She doesn't deserve any consideration at all. The tales about her haven't been exaggerated, that's not difficult to see.'

'But what's going to happen to her?' Gail spoke dejectedly, almost to herself.

'Why should you care?'

'Because it's a terrible thing, Heather, when you see a young girl ruining her life and you're helpless to do anything about it.'

An exasperated sigh from Heather and then she said practically,

'For the time being, forget her and let's enjoy ourselves. Will you put the basket in the car, and tell those scamps we're ready. I'm just going upstairs to fetch my handbag.'

Heather drove Roger's car, taking the road to Killiecrankie and then following the shores of lovely Loch Tummel, where towering conifers often overshadowed the road, spilling down from the smooth dark hills which rose on both sides of the loch.

'Can we stop?' asked Manda as they neared the western end of the loch. 'We want to play in the woods.'

'Stop? Already?' They had covered no more than twenty miles. 'Aren't you enjoying the ride?'

'Yes, but we want to play a bit.'

'What do you say, Gail?'

'It's nice here. I think we'll let them get out and run off some of their energy.'

'I might have known,' laughed Heather. 'You'll spoil those two before you've done.'

'I don't think so,' returned Gail with confidence.

She and Heather drank their coffee on the bank while the four children played noisily in the woods.

'It casts a spell on you,' murmured Heather after a long silence between them.

'It's certainly cast a spell on me.' Gail fell silent again, staring dreamily around. The wooded slopes and heathered moorland pastures; the heights of Doire Leathan and Tairnechan and Craig Chean forming part of the watershed from which numerous little burns came foaming down to join the still clear waters of Loch Tummel; the loch itself, with its bright green banks and little odd-shaped promontories; the profound awareness of colour—purples and blues, and a bewildering number of greens blended with the skill and perfection only Nature can achieve.

'It must be fantastic in winter,' Heather was saying. 'I hope we have snow at Christmas.'

'I'm sure we shall.' Gail was waiting eagerly for the spectacle of grandeur despite Sinclair's warnings of the severity and bleakness of a Highland winter. True, there would be times when icy mists would swirl across the moors and frowning ominous clouds would wrap their cloak of darkness round the hills, but there would be the good days—days of breathtaking wonder when the sun in a clear blue sky would touch the brilliant white snow with gold, when frost-draped trees would sparkle and shimmer in the glen and the roar of the burn would become no more than a murmur under its covering of ice. There would be days when the fresh clear air would intoxicate and days when the winds would blow sharply over the moors ... 'winds austere and pure'.

'Do you want to drive?' Heather's voice brought Gail back from her pleasant musings and she smiled.

'I was miles away! No, I don't want to drive. It's nice to be driven for a change.'

Heather glanced oddly at her. 'Andrew doesn't take you out?'

Reluctantly Gail shook her head. 'He hasn't a great deal of time,' was all she said, but Heather's next words echoed her thoughts.

'A man in his position could make time, were he so inclined. He seems to have enough men employed on the estate.'

This was true. Andrew had seven farm hands, two foresters and two gamekeepers in addition to the joiner and mason and, of course, his estate manager, Sinclair.

'He likes working,' submitted Gail after a pause, and then changed the subject, asking Heather if she would like to go south, to Loch Tay, or carry on along the valley towards Loch Rannoch.

'I don't mind. We'll go a little further along this road; it looks attractive.' Heather called to the children and they all got into the car.

'It's a very pretty road; I'm glad we took it.' Gail had driven to Loch Rannoch one day on her own, after taking the children to school. 'We can have our lunch somewhere on the loch side.'

The heights rose all around, with the prominent Ben Chaullaich to the north and the resistant quartzite summit of the graceful Schiehallion dominating the landscape to the south.

'That's the Sugar Loaf Mountain,' Robbie informed his companions. 'You think it's snow on top, don't you? But it isn't.'

After travelling along for some time by a wooded hillside they entered a wider part of the valley, coming to the charming village of Kinloch Rannoch. On leaving it behind they came upon wilder territory, where the complex nature and scale of the faulting and contortion of the rocks gave a greater diversity of landscape. There were more crags, and the valleys were for the most part deep defiles between ridges of high land.

However, after travelling about five miles alongside the loch they reached gentler country again, with soft rolling hills coming almost down to the shore on both sides of the loch.

'Can we go round to the other side of the loch?' Robbie leant forward to speak to Gail. 'Mummy, can we go to Black Wood?'

'Black Wood?' echoed Manda. 'That sounds creepy!'

'It is creepy, isn't it, Mummy? The trees are dark and so close together that it's all shadowy inside the woods, and there are ghosts!'

'Ghosts?' Manda spoke in an awed voice, and shuddered. 'I don't want to go, then.'

'There aren't any ghosts, Manda,' laughed Gail. 'Robbie's only teasing you.'

'Are you, Robbie?' asked Simon, disappointed.

'Well. . . .' he began, then saw Gail's expression. 'Yes,' he owned, grinning, 'I was only teasing—about the ghosts, that is. But the wood's creepy, isn't it, Mummy?'

'Yes, I'll admit it is. Do you others want to go?' she then asked.

'The boys do and the girls don't,' submitted Robbie. 'But the boys are older, so they have the pick.'

'Do they, now?' from Heather. 'And what gave you the idea that because you're older you should have the pick?'

'It's only fair,' put in Simon.

'The fair way is to vote.'

'Yes, that's fair,' said Shena eagerly. 'You and Mummy are girls, so we'll have the most votes.'

'Certainly we'll have the most votes.'

'I shall vote with the boys,' promised Gail as they both gave dissatisfied little grunts.

'In that case,' laughed Heather, 'we'll have our pic-

143

nic on this side of the loch and then go over to the other side.'

No sunlight entered the Black Wood of Rannoch, relic of the ancient Caledonian Forest where wolves once freely roamed, because the firs were tall and thick and very close together. But despite its density all four children entered, the boys making weird howls as they raced on ahead.

Gail and Heather then played hide and seek with them until at last they all piled into the car and made for home.

'We've had a marvellous time!' Robbie told his father. 'You should have come with us; it was *super*!'

Catching his wife's eye, Andrew smiled, but it was a forced smile, produced for the benefit of Heather and Roger and one or two other guests who happened to be there.

'We went into Black Wood,' Simon gave this piece of information as he drew a not very clean handkerchief from his pocket. Out fell a knot of dirty string, two rusty nails, a few small sweets and several crumpled snapshots.

'Simon!' cried his mother. 'What——? The way that child shows me up!' She made a helpless gesture with her hands. 'The things he puts in his pockets—and just look at the colour of that handkerchief!'

Everyone else laughed, as much at Heather as at her son. Stooping, Andrew picked up the snapshots ... and instantly his attention was arrested.

'Where did you get those?' Heather was standing by Andrew and she glanced at one of the pictures in his hand.

'You were sorting out one day and you threw them away, saying they were no good—you said those of Gran were awful, and so were those of Auntie Gail and her boy-friends. Don't you remember?' He blew his nose loudly and began stuffing the handkerchief back into his pocket. 'You kept some others because they were nicer. I didn't like those going in the dustbin,' he added, getting up on tiptoe in order to take a look. 'So I took them out of the waste-paper basket and put them in my pocket.'

After flicking through them with assumed carelessness Andrew passed the snapshots to Heather and, his gaze meeting that of his wife, he noted the sudden flush which had risen to her cheeks.

It was the following morning before he found himself alone with her and was able to put the questions she guessed he had been wanting to ask.

'Who was the man you were sunbathing with?'

'He—he was my fiancé—' Gail twisted her hands together. It was a totally unconscious gesture, but one portraying nervousness, and a frown settled on her husband's brow.

'You've been engaged? You never mentioned it.'

A wan little smile touched her lips.

'We didn't have much time to confide in one another,' she reminded him gently.

'You broke the engagement?' Andrew looked at her through narrowed eyes.

Gail hesitated, but because she was completely honest she said,

'No, Michael broke the engagement.'

'He did?' sharply, and with a quick and questioning raising of his brows. 'Why?'

Suspicion again, no doubt of that. Should she tell him the whole? But no, for somehow she had always considered her inability to have children as a stigma, putting her on a plane below the level of other women. Had Andrew loved her she could have told him, but he did not love her, and at the forefront of her mind were the words Morag had spoken about his never tolerating anything inferior. True, he had once chided Gail for entertaining the idea of her own inferiority, when she had been so reluctant to tell him of the scar on her shoulder, but at that time he had been in a totally different mood from that in which he was at present.

'I prefer to keep the reason to myself,' she told him

unhappily at last. His eyes raked, contempt in their depths. Obviously he inferred from her evasion that the blame had been hers, that Michael had had some valid reason for breaking the engagement.

'You had been engaged some time?'

'Almost a year.'

He paused a moment.

'The accident you mentioned—it must have occurred after that snapshot was taken?'

'It did, yes—a few months afterwards.'

What was he thinking? she wondered. Perhaps that she had been out with another man when the accident had happened, and that was the reason for the broken engagement? The idea was like a piercing dart of agony and she wanted to tell him everything, but before she could make up her mind he was speaking again.

'The other snapshot—who was that man you were with?' Andrew's voice was edged with condemnation, his manner that of a judge. Gail felt her temper rise, crushing any desire she might have had to vindicate herself.

'What I did before I met you is my own affair!' she flashed at him. 'I don't inquire into your past, and you've no right to inquire into mine!'

CHAPTER NINE

HER words did nothing to improve the position, and it was with a sense of dread that she watched the car drive away, carrying her sister and her family from her ... leaving her alone with Andrew. No such sense of dread and dejection had occurred on the previous occasion, but at that time Gail had been filled with optimism for the future, clinging to the hope that one day Andrew would turn to her, his bitterness and hurt dissolved. He might fall in love with her, Gail had confidently said to Beth, but with the qualifying, 'If my stars up there just keep going in their present direction'. Well, her stars had not kept going in their present direction, and now Gail was forced to accept the fact that the happiness she derived from Shena and Robbie was all she would ever experience. And indeed this would have been all she desired, and more, had she not foolishly fallen in love with her husband. Beth had called her a chump, Heather had said she was crazy—and they were right.

But Gail was ever grateful for the opportunity of loving, and being loved by, Shena and Robbie, and as the weeks passed she discovered that with resignation, with the acceptance of her fate, she was acquiring a sense of peace, becoming alive to the beauty around her as the seasons began their first almost imperceptible change and the warm soft colours of autumn appeared, first in the high places and then spreading down to the lower ground. There was the russet of bracken among the green hill slopes, the red of the mountain ash in the glen; there were golds and browns and yellows even while the heather remained purple on the moors.

And at this time of the year there were the captivating little fawns, dappled and full of life, bounding along by their mothers. A few weeks ago they had been neglected, for during the rutting season the does were otherwise occupied. But a fawn would never be too far from its mother, even at that time, merely grazing at a safe distance from the buck, who could be decidedly unfriendly towards it—though it would never actually harm it. But towards the doe the roebuck had a deep fidelity, being monogamous, unlike the red deer stag who, with his herd of does, would often have to fight another stag who challenged his right of possession.

'What I can't understand,' said Gail one day to Sinclair, with whom she was always able to speak more freely than with her husband, 'is that although the rutting season for the roe is in August, and that of the red deer in October, the fawns are all born in June.'

'Some are born in May—the roe, that is,' he said. 'But the majority come in June, as you say, at the same time as the red deer. The reason is that there's a sort of delayed action with the roe——'

'Delayed action?'

'It's more technically described as "delayed implantation". The animals mate, but there follows a period of dormancy until December, when normal development begins.' He smiled and shook his head in a reflective sort of way. 'Nature's very strange at times, Mrs. MacNeill. The safest month for these little creatures to be born in the Highlands is of course June—and that's when they are born—at the same time as the red deer and the sika deer. Odd, isn't it?'

'It's wonderful, and mysterious,' she breathed. 'As you say, Nature's very strange at times.'

While these beautiful little fawns were a delight to Gail the month of September was marred somewhat because then it was that the sporting highlight of the year began—the stalking of the red deer stags.

However, she was coming round gradually to the acceptance of the shooting, Sinclair having talked seriously to her about the danger of over-population of the deer in the Highlands. The stalker would always advise the 'rifle' which stags to shoot. Old and sickly animals must always be killed for the ultimate good of the herd. He said much the same as Andrew had said, but in a gentler, more patient sort of way. If the stalking was done with skill and with concern for the animal, it did not know it was being pursued and, therefore, suffered no apprehension or fear. If the kill was clean it suffered no pain.

But Sinclair admitted that the kill was not always clean. Nevertheless, it was an unwritten law that a wounded animal must be followed and secured, even if this meant the ruining of the rest of the day's sport for both stalker and 'rifle'.

'A wounded beast is a great anxiety to everyone until it's secured,' the factor went on to add. 'And you'll find that most lairds allow only marksmen on their land.'

The stag stalking took place on one of his other estates further north, but for some reason Andrew did not go. Gail naturally did not ask him why, because nothing personal ever entered into the conversation, but Morag one day provided the answer.

'He won't go away because he thinks I'll be off! I hate him—and I've told him so! He always goes up there in September, and I never thought he'd forgo his sport just to remain on guard over me.' She paced the floor, her eyes blazing. She had been up and about for some weeks and appeared to be perfectly well again. Gail sensed her desire to be off and had herself kept a watch on her whenever possible. But of course Gail had to be out for part of the day, when she was taking Robbie and Shena to school or bringing them home. It seemed as if Andrew had also guessed at Morag's desire to go away, and this time he was quite determined to keep her at home, even at the expense of his own recreation and pleasure. Morag's allowance had been stopped, but Andrew gave her small amounts of money now and then. She would buy cigarettes—all those in the house having been put out of her way—and smoke

149

them, as she always had, when her father was not about. 'I'll get away,' threatened Morag, coming to a halt before Gail. 'As soon as I can get hold of enough money I'm off! He can't keep a watch on me all the time; it isn't possible!'

'You know that whatever he does it's for your own good. You're still not well, Morag, and therefore——'

'I'm perfectly well! I know how I feel, and I've never been better. But I'll be ill if I have to stick much more of this—ill in my mind. I'll go mad!'

Gail let the matter drop, unwilling to be disturbed by Morag's tantrums, and the normal routine continued—Gail being absorbed with the children, Andrew with his work, and Morag remaining as a stranger in the house, scarcely speaking to the children and rarely appearing at the table at meal times.

'There's something evil about that girl,' Heather had said on one occasion during her last stay at Dunlochrie House, but Gail now wondered if the girl suffered from some abnormality of the brain. She had hinted at this in a recent letter to Heather, and the reply, sharp and to the point, was that Gail was altogether too soft. Morag was bad, and this was by her own volition and not the result of some misfortune.

Robin had never come to the loch since Gail's last quarrel with Andrew and she knew he had carried out his threat and forbidden Robin to fish in the loch. Gail had not seen Robin for several weeks, but she knew that inevitably she must do so one day, as he lived not so very far away, and she dreaded the meeting, for embarrassing questions would naturally be put to her by Robin. The meeting occurred as she was coming out of the village sweet shop. He greeted her, looked at the car standing on the road, and asked her to give him a lift. She could scarcely refuse without an excuse and reluctantly she invited him to get in. And she knew immediately he opened his mouth that the request for a lift had been made with the deliberate intention of questioning her.

'Gail, what happened when I was up last time? Your husband was so short and stiff the next time I came, and he told me I was not to use the loch again—or ever to come to the house. I hadn't done anything wrong that I could see—just having talked to Morag for a while and then gone about my business. I borrowed the boat, it's true, but the factor gave me permission to do so.' Gail did not answer at once and he continued, 'I have average intelligence, Gail, and I could see at once that your husband's manner portrayed all the evidence of a deep and furious resentment of me. What have I done?'

Gail started the car, shaking her head in refusal as he offered her a cigarette.

'Didn't you ask him?' she parried, searching for a way of avoiding anything personal entering the conversation.

'Ask him!' The exclamation was accompanied by a lifting of his brows. 'No, I did not. Your husband was in no mood to be questioned by anyone like me. But you must know what it's all about. What have I done?' he repeated.

She considered for a while and then decided frankness was the best policy. In any case, she felt he was owed an explanation and she told him what Morag had done. To her surprise the expected outburst did not come and she realized her candour had been a mistake as he said slowly and with emphasis,

'Well, Gail, Morag was right. I liked you the moment I set eyes on you——'

'Robin, please——'

'You've been frank with me and I'll be equally frank with you,' he went on, ignoring the interruption. 'It's all over the village that Andrew MacNeill decided that a mother for his children was preferable to a nanny, because he'd never been able to keep a nanny, and also because he had got it into his head that his children would grow up feeling they were different—having no mother.' A small pause, but Gail could find nothing to

151

say, being aware only of the humiliation that was sweeping over her at the idea of this unflattering gossip concerning her position at Dunlochrie House. 'Is this true? But I've really no need to ask, Gail, because Andrew MacNeill would never fall in love—he hasn't got it in him to love; he's too hard. Gail, this sort of life isn't for you!'

They had reached a lonely byroad and Gail turned into it, stopping the car after drawing on to a grass verge.

'Robin,' she said, turning in her seat, 'you don't know me well enough for this kind of talk. The total length of time we've spent in each other's company can't amount to more than a few hours——'

'Time! What is time?' he interrupted, reaching out to take her hand, but she withdrew it swiftly from the steering wheel. 'Why do you think I wanted to come up to the loch? To see you, of course—but you seemed always to avoid me.'

She gave an anxious glance around her, afraid they would be seen by someone who might casually mention the matter to her husband.

'Andrew has forbidden me to speak to you,' she told Robin quietly at last. 'And after what you've just said I've decided to heed his wishes. Obviously it's common knowledge what he's been through, and I shall be the last one to bring further hurt and humiliation to him.'

'You're not going to speak to me again? Not even *speak*?' He stared at her in disbelief. 'But the laird's wife is expected to be friendly with everyone; her position demands it. The laird himself is the kingpin of the village and people bring their problems to him. He and his wife are friends to them all; you've been here long enough to know that.'

'You've made it impossibe for me to be your friend,' Gail reluctantly told him. 'I'm married, Robin, and quite content with my life, no matter what the gossip might be.'

A silence ensued, but from outside came the fierce

roar of a tumbling burn as it sped on its way to join the valley of the Tilt.

'You're ... angry with me?' Robin spoke at last, staring straight ahead.

'I'm certainly not pleased at the way you've spoken to me. I've never given you the slightest encouragement and wouldn't ever do so. As I said, I'm quite content with my life.'

He looked at her long and hard.

'I don't believe you!' Gail merely threw him a rather haughty glance and he shrugged his shoulders resignedly. 'So you're going to pass me by whenever we meet?' Gail nodded and he said, 'Do you want me to get out here?'

'If you please, Robin. It's better if you do; someone might see us.'

'In the ordinary way no one would give the matter a second thought. It's nothing unusual for the laird or his wife to offer a lift to one of the villagers.'

'In the ordinary way no one would give the matter a second thought,' Gail agreed readily, but added, 'However, the present circumstances are far from ordinary.' She switched on the engine; Robin stubbed his cigarette in the ash tray, got out of the car, and walked away without a backward glance.

Gail continued some distance along the deserted lane, her nerves tensed and her heart beating a little too quickly. There had been something sordid about the conversation in which she had been engaged just now, for it would seem Robin was more than ready to indulge in a flirtation with her. His attitude had lacked the respect due to the laird's wife and she experienced a feeling of shame, just as if she *had* given him encouragement—which of course she hadn't, as she so firmly reminded him.

On reaching the end of the lane she stopped the car and got out, revelling in the feel of frosty air on her face and in her nostrils. The dawning had been grey, glowering over the stark Highland landscape, but with increasing light the indeterminate skyline cleared as the drifting mist succumbed to the onslaught of the sun. Vast areas of parkland and estate forests lay to her right, while to her left lay sterner country—the wild solitude of the moors and dark immensity of the distant heights, deeply dissected by the Garry and its numerous tributaries.

Presently Gail drove away, calmer now and refreshed in mind and body by the heady air and the vast stillness which had surrounded her as she stood there beside the car, absorbing all that was clean and pure, and wondering at the magic hand that wrought such splendour on the trees—the short-lived splendour of rose and gold, and bronze, for the leaves were falling swiftly now and soon the parklands and the forests would be dominated by the dull green foliage of the pines and firs rising gauntly to a sombre winter sky.

It was a week later that Andrew used the car. He did not smoke himself, and used the ash tray only as a receptacle for odd bits of paper and items like parking fee tickets. It was on depositing one of these in the ash tray that he noticed the half-smoked cigarette which Robin had left when in angry haste he had stubbed it before leaving the car. The first Gail knew of this was when he broached the subject by a preliminary inquiry.

'Do you smoke?'

'Of course not.' She stared at him, puzzled. 'You know I don't smoke.'

'Has Morag used the small car?'

She shook her head. What was he getting at?

'No, she uses the runabout.' Morag loved driving and would spend hours going round the estate roads in the runabout. 'No one uses the small car except me—and you, occasionally, of course.'

He regarded her through half-closed eyes, his features harsh and accusing.

'Then who,' he inquired softly, 'left the half-smoked cigarette in the ash tray?'

Gail caught her breath. She had made a mental note of the presence of the cigarette, intending to remove it—but the matter had slipped her memory. And now, in her anxiety to prevent a further deterioration in their relationship, she said flounderingly,

'I do smoke sometimes, and I probably left it there——'

'Don't lie! You've had that man in the car—in *my* car!'

White-faced and trembling, she admitted to giving Robin a lift, and at the dark and almost murderous expression coming over her husband's face she went on swiftly to say she had told Robin she wasn't ever going to speak to him again. Contrary to her expectations her submission to Andrew's wishes did not have the desired effect.

'You actually discussed me with him——?'

'Oh, no, Andrew——'

'You must have! There would have to be some sort of talk, otherwise how did you come to the point of telling him you wouldn't speak to him again?'

'I had to explain why I couldn't speak to him,' she began unhappily. 'I couldn't just cut him dead as you wanted me to. But I didn't say very much at all.'

His mouth went tight, and at the look he gave her she was plunged into misery. His cold indifference she had come to accept and endure, but this suspicion, this icy contempt springing from the conviction that she had discussed him with a young man from the village ... these she could not bear, and in a little beseeching gesture she spread her hands, opening her mouth to speak, anxious to placate him, but he was before her.

'That you could openly discuss me with this man, endeavour to humiliate me——'

'Andrew, I didn't!' She shook her head, tears filling her eyes. 'Why should you think I'd try to humiliate you? What good would it do me?' She took a halting step towards him. 'If only I could make you understand I don't ever want to hurt you then you wouldn't

155

suspect me as you do.' She looked up into his face, her eyes wide and filmed, distorting her vision. 'You asked me not to speak to Robin again, and I'm willing to observe your wishes. Surely we can now let the matter drop—and never bring it up again.'

She was close to him, and in a little dejected movement she had allowed her outstretched hands to drop to her sides. Whether it was this which effected a softening in him, or whether it was the pleading sincerity of her words she would never know, but he did soften—not to any great extent, it was true, but at least his fury dissolved and the harshness faded from his eyes.

'Very well, Gail, we won't speak of the matter again.' But he did not apologize for his unkind accusations, or provide any indication that he would have liked to withdraw them.

And life from then on continued as before, still in an atmosphere of coldness and total lack of interest, with Andrew becoming human only when Robbie and Shena were there—at teatimes and on Sunday morning when they all went to church, and later when they took their customary walk, which they did in all weathers, except of course in heavy rain.

When the half-term break came in October, Gail, feeling the necessity of a change which would give her frayed nerves a rest, asked Andrew if she could go and stay with Beth for the week.

'It would be a nice change for Robbie and Shena,' she added, and as his brows shot up in surprise she guessed at once that he'd concluded she wanted to go alone.

'You indicated just now that you needed a rest,' he said, a difficult and unexpected smile touching his lips. 'You won't have much of a rest if you take the children.'

'I wouldn't go without them,' she returned simply.

He regarded her in silence for a space, cold and unemotional, it seemed ... except for the movement of a muscle in his cheek.

'Very well. Do you want to take the car?'

'If it's all right with you. Otherwise we can go on the train. Beth or Harvey will meet us at the other end.'

'Use the train then,' he said. 'It's a long way to drive, and the children are sure to get troublesome.'

She smiled at him, wondering if his concern was as genuine as it sounded, or whether his suggestion of using the train was merely a manifestation of his usual practicality of mind.

Andrew drove them to the station and saw them on to the train, buying books and chocolates for them all. As the train moved off he waved; the children hung out of the window and waved furiously until their father was eventually lost to view. Then they sat down, opening their books, but Gail remained by the window until the train passed the end of the last curving building. Andrew was walking to his car and, as if suddenly conscious of being watched, he glanced up. Gail waved and he waved back. She thought he smiled at her, but at this distance she could not be sure.

Beth met the train and within half an hour Gail was once again in the home to which she had come on the death of her mother. Thomas and Marilyn were also on holiday from school and immediately took Robbie and Shena off to play in the garden.

'So you can have a cup of tea in peace,' said Thomas obligingly after suggesting that they all go outside.

'Come in as soon as it rains,' said his mother. 'It looks as if it'll come down any minute now.'

'It's like old times!' The eagerness in Gail's voice brought her sister's head up with a jerk, and she said slowly,

'Aren't you happy, Gail?'

'Happy? Of course I'm happy. Why should you ask that?'

'No need to hedge.' Beth poured Gail a cup of tea. 'Heather didn't seem to think things were as good as they might be between you and Andrew.'

'I expect she told you everything?'

'She did. And it seems to me someone should do something about that Morag. Can't she be put in a home or something?'

Gail blinked. 'What for?'

'To keep the little bitch out of mischief ... and to prevent her from making mischief. Why should she want to break up your marriage?'

'She wasn't exactly trying to break it up. I often think she's so bored she does anything just to relieve the monotony,' Gail added after a slight pause.

'She wouldn't be bored if she'd go to school. I thought you said Andrew was sending her in September?'

'He arranged for her to go to boarding school, yes. But then she was ill, and the doctor doesn't now advise it. He says she should be at home.'

'Well, if she's to be there all the time I don't see how you and Andrew are going to get together. She'll come between you all the time, with her lies and deceit and mischief-making.'

Gail helped herself to sugar and began stirring her tea.

'I've given up hoping that Andrew and I will ever get together,' she admitted at length. 'This is the way he wants it—nothing but a business arrangement.' She glanced at her sister across the table. 'He won't ever love me, Beth. I was a fool to cherish such a stupid idea.'

Beth frowned.

'You were not so pessimistic the last time I saw you,' she reminded her grimly, and it was easy to see that her thoughts were still on Morag. 'In fact, you were right up in the air—pretty sure he'd fall for you in time.'

Rain began to splash on the window and the four children came rushing in.

'The playroom, if you please,' said Beth crisply. 'We haven't had our tea yet.'

'I've just said I was a fool,' Gail reminded her when

the children had gone. 'You see, he never once gave me the slightest reason for my hopes.' She smiled, rather sadly. 'He kissed me once, but now I come to think of it it wasn't really a kiss—just a sort of comforting gesture.' He had kissed her twice, she recalled, but somehow Gail had attached more importance to the first occasion. Beth was looking inquiringly at her and Gail went into a little more detail about what happened when her scar was revealed.

Beth's eyes took on a strange expression and when Gail at last became silent she murmured in a soft and thoughtful tone,

'Why should he have wanted to comfort you? Have you never asked yourself that?' And as Gail shook her head, her glance uncomprehending, Beth went on, 'You'd just had a big row and then suddenly he becomes kind and kisses you. Was all this part of the "business arrangement" he entered into with you?'

'I don't know what you're getting at, Beth?'

'If it hadn't been for that spiteful wretch poisoning his mind, and bringing back all he's gone through with his first wife you and Andrew would have been together by now,' Beth declared emphatically, her eyes hard and narrowed. 'But you'll make no headway with that girl around, as I've just said. Can't you persuade Andrew to send her to school?'

'The doctor won't allow it, Beth,' returned Gail with slight impatience. 'No, Morag must stay at home.'

'She's not only a barrier between you and Andrew, but she's also a barrier to his peace of mind.'

Gail said nothing, but she recalled having thought the very thing that Beth had just put into words. Morag was a barrier to Andrew's peace of mind. And without complete peace of mind he could never begin to seek for happiness ... even should he wish to seek for it.

'Perhaps,' sighed Gail in a half-hearted sort of way, 'she'll get married in a few years' time.'

'Well, if it weren't that I'd be delighted for your

159

sake, I'd never, *never* wish that one on the son of my worst enemy!'

Before Gail could make any remark on that the children came to the door, standing by it as if afraid of entering the room.

'We're awful hungry,' complained Thomas, looking at the biscuits on the tray. 'Shena and Robbie haven't had anything to eat for hours and hours!'

Gail looked at her nephew with amused perception.

'All right, your mummy and I will make you something at once. Go and wash your faces and hands and when you've done that your tea will be ready.'

'I've an appointment at the hairdressers tomorrow,' Beth said as they were cutting the children's sandwiches. 'I always go on Tuesdays because they're slack. Both Thomas and Marilyn want hair-cuts, so would you like to look around town and we'll all meet and have lunch somewhere? I could cancel the hair-do,' she went on to say, when Gail interrupted her.

'No, don't do that. I'd love to go round the shops. I've missed them, and so it'll be a nice change. Perhaps I'll get a dress from Anita—I've never been able to get anything as nice as hers. She seems to have exactly what suits me.'

'Anita knows how to buy,' said Beth. 'She's expensive, though, so you naturally expect the best.'

Beth dropped Gail and the two children in the main street and then went to park the car. They would all meet at the Grand Hotel, where they were to have lunch.

'Can we buy you a present, Mummy?' Shena asked, holding on to Gail's hand and trotting along beside her.

'I want to buy a present as well,' put in Robbie, who was holding her sister's other hand. 'And I want to buy something for Daddy and Morag.'

'I was just going to suggest you buy them something. Do that first, and then if you've any money left you can buy me something.'

'I want to buy yours first, and then Daddy's, and then Morag's—— Oh, Mummy, look!' Shena dragged them both towards a shop window. 'Handbags! Do you want a new handbag?'

'You haven't got that much money,' interposed Robbie on a little scornful note.

'I have!—haven't I, Mummy?'

'I don't need a handbag, darling. Shall we go into the big store and look around? We'll have lots more choice there.'

The children each bought Andrew a little blown glass animal for his study 'so he can look at them when he's working', Robbie had told the smiling assistant. For Morag they bought a bottle of perfume between them—and subsidised by Gail, without their knowledge. For Gail Shena had bought a little French doll for her dressing-table and Robbie bought her a small picture with bright red roses tumbling all about the walls of a quaint little thatched cottage.

After buying presents for all four children Gail suggested they then pool to buy something for Auntie Beth.

Eventually Gail was able to go to her favourite dress shop and to her satisfaction she managed to buy a pretty day dress in soft lambswool, and a cocktail dress with just the right length of sleeve to hide the scar, and no more.

'You look beautiful!' exclaimed Robbie enthusiastically. 'Are you going to wear it tonight?'

'Not tonight, Robbie. When I go to a party, perhaps.'

'Can I carry it for you?' Shena asked as they came out of the shop.

'No, thank you, Shena. It's rather a big box and I think I'd better carry it. Besides, you have all your other parcels.'

They had about ten minutes to spare and were idly looking in shop windows when Gail twisted round abruptly on hearing her name called.

'Michael ... how are you?' She smiled, noting his interest in Robbie and Shena.

'I'm fine, Gail.' A small pause and then, 'You're married, I hear.'

She nodded, her smile deepening. Not the merest grudge did she now bear him. His action had helped to shape her life and she was glad she was not married to him.

'This is Robbie, and this is Shena,' she said as he continued to stare down at them.

'You married a—divorced man?'

'My husband's first wife died some years ago.'

'Oh, sorry. The children are young. I naturally concluded that their mother would be still living. Sorry,' he said again, and added, 'Just heard it casually— about your marriage, I mean, and no one seemed to know anything, except that your husband had children—it was three, I thought?'

'He has another daughter. She's much older.' Gail did not expand on that and Michael went on to say he supposed they were staying at Beth's. 'Yes, that's right. The children are off school, so it was a good opportunity to come.'

He looked her over, noting her expensive clothes and also those of the children.

'Your husband ... he's Scottish, I seem to have heard?'

She had to smile. Michael's curiosity amused her. But she also felt a certain pride in her position and as she was only human she said, with a little touch of dignity,

'He's the Laird of Dunlochrie.'

'My, but that sounds grand! Do you live in a big house?'

'Yes, it's very big,' put in Robbie suddenly, smiling up at Michael. 'But it has to be big because lots of people live in it and because sometimes Daddy has lots of visitors staying, doesn't he, Mummy?'

'Lots of people live with you?' asked Michael, affording Gail no opportunity of answering Robbie's question.

'Yes—we have Mummy and Daddy and me and Shena and Morag. And then we have three maids, and Mrs. Birchan——'

'Robbie!' laughed Gail. 'Mr. Bankfoot doesn't want to know all that.'

'But he asked if lots of people lived with us. Shall I tell him about all the men, then?'

'No, darling.' She glanced at her watch. 'We must be going,' she said to Michael. 'We've to meet Beth in a few minutes.'

'I was going to ask you to join me for lunch. I use the café over the road, there.'

'Thank you, Michael, but we can't. How are your little ones, by the way? I haven't been able to get a word in to ask,' she apologized with a smile.

'Fine, just fine.'

'Good. Remember me to Joan, won't you?'

'I will.'

'Goodbye—we must hurry. Say goodbye, Robbie and Shena.'

'Goodbye,' they said, turning to wave as they walked away from Michael.

'Who was that, Mummy?' Shena asked.

'An old friend. . . .' Her voice trailed off and she frowned. With her husband's ever-present suspicions in mind she was always on her guard these days. Would Robbie or Shena mention this encounter? It was all wrong that Gail should have to worry over it, but she did worry. And yet she shrugged, for there was nothing she could do about it. Should either Robbie or Shena talk to Andrew of the meeting with Michael then it would be just too bad. She, Gail, would tell him the truth, as she always did, saying it was merely a chance meeting lasting no more than five minutes or so. And if he happened to be in the mood to make a scene then it would just have to be borne, as all the other scenes had been borne.

CHAPTER TEN

THEY returned to Dunlochrie on the Saturday, Gail being unwilling to be away from home on Sunday. It was the day they were together as a family and a day which they all thoroughly enjoyed.

Andrew met them at the station and for the entire half hour which the homeward journey took Robbie and Shena chattered, relating every detail that to them had seemed important, but to Gail's relief no mention was made of the encounter with her ex-fiancé.

'Did you miss us?' asked Robbie as the thought suddenly struck him.

'I missed you very much, Robbie.' The words were spoken with unusual gentleness, and on an almost tremulous note which startled Gail, not having witnessed in her husband anything remotely akin to tender emotion. A product of the Highlands, he always seemed to reflect the harshness of the environment in which he had been born and reared.

'We missed you, didn't we, Mummy?' Shena took hold of Gail's hand as she leant forward to press a kiss on her father's cheek. 'Why didn't you come with us?'

'I had work to do, Shena.'

'Will you come next time?' urged Robbie. 'It's nicer with us all—just like this.'

Curiously, Gail half-turned in her seat, recalling for some obscure reason, the incident when she stayed by the compartment window and waved to Andrew as he crossed towards his car. He had waved back ... and she'd had the impression that he smiled at her. He was not smiling now and his profile was as firm and set as ever—and yet his lips were soft, his whole manner pensive as he kept his eyes on the road ahead. It was long and straight, cutting right through the moorlands. Dotted here and there were small clumps of trees, clear indications of bygone habitation. But the trees themselves were all that remained of those lonely steadings whose owners toiled and sweated in their endeavour to eke out a living from the unyielding land.

Aware of her gaze upon him, he turned—and the heart seemed suddenly to be wrenched right out of Gail. He'd been lonely! The revelation staggered her ... and at the same time stirred her profoundly, for it appeared in some strange way to provide an opening for an improvement in their relationship.

'Robbie and I have bought you presents,' Shena was saying. 'Robbie's is a nice——'

'It's a surprise,' Robbie hastily cut in.

'Why? I want to tell Daddy about our presents.'

'You should wait till we get home, and then he'll have a surprise when he opens them.'

'But——'

'If Robbie wants his present to be a surprise,' interrupted Gail gently, 'then just tell Daddy what you've bought for him.'

'But we've both bought the same.'

'Did you have to tell him?' demanded Robbie, clicking his tongue impatiently. 'Now you *can't* say what you've bought!'

'They're not both exactly the same.' Shena leant forward again, over Andrew's shoulder. 'Mine's blue and Robbie's is green. Which colour do you like best?'

'I like them both the same,' was the grave reply as Andrew turned off the main road and took the narrower one leading to the village.

'Stop her from telling Daddy—please, Mummy. I want my present to be a surprise—and she's going to say what it is. I know she is!'

'You mustn't, Shena.' Gail urged her back and made her sit down. 'We'll be home in a few minutes; surely you can wait that long.'

'All right, I'll wait.'

'It's because she's young that she has no patience,' commented Robbie scathingly, and both Gail and Andrew laughed.

'Tell me about Beth,' he invited. 'You haven't been able to get a word in yet.'

Gail talked casually about their holiday, wondering as she cast him a glance now and then whether his interest was real, or merely assumed for the sake of politeness.

'Do you like your presents?' Shena was asking a short while later as they all sat in the snug.

'That's the third time you've asked Daddy if he likes his presents,' said Robbie. 'Of course he likes them.' So serious he was, thought Gail, a small sigh issuing from her lips. He was becoming quite mature for his age; she hoped he wasn't going to grow up too quickly.

But the next moment he was just a little boy again as he eagerly invited his sister to join in a game with him.

'We haven't played it yet,' he told his father. 'Mummy bought it for us and we had no time to play it at Auntie Beth's because we went out every day.'

'It seems to me,' laughed Andrew, 'that you've all been spending a good deal of your time buying presents for everybody else.'

'It was only one morning, when Auntie Beth went to have her hair done. We three went shopping——'

'And we saw a nice man who wanted to take us to lunch,' put in Shena brightly. 'He was a friend of Mummy's.'

Both Gail and Andrew looked up, and their eyes met.

'It was Michael,' she said calmly, resigned to unpleasantness while hoping desperately she could pass this matter off without it.

'Michael?' he frowned.

'You saw a snapshot of him. . . .'

'Yes, I remember. You were once engaged to him.'

'He's married, with three young children,' she submitted in a low voice.

'You didn't go to lunch with him, apparently.' No hardness in his tone. This was merely conversation, even though it was, on Andrew's part, carried on with the sole object of extracting information from Gail about her ex-fiancé.

'No, we hadn't time. We were meeting Beth at the Grand.'

'And if you hadn't been meeting Beth?'

'I wouldn't have accepted his invitation.' It suddenly struck her that the last time Michael's name was mentioned she had flared into a temper, telling Andrew he had no right to inquire into her past. A widening of the rift between them had resulted and she had no desire that the same thing should happen again. 'Michael and I have nothing in common any more.'

'You're still friends, nevertheless?'

She smiled reflectively. 'It would be more apt to say we are not enemies.'

He continued to look at her, but after a while he turned away, picking up one of the little glass animals and twisting it in his hand, absently allowing it to catch the light from the fire so that the colour changed and deepened. Gail leant back in her chair, watching him with a lightening heart. He had by his dropping of the subject revealed to her the first signs of trust.

She herself had bought Andrew a present, although the children had not seen her get it. She postponed giving it to him until Robbie and Shena were in bed, and even then she hesitated, feeling shy and reluctant because of the previous coldness existing between them right up to the moment of her departure for Beth's.

But as he sat there, on the opposite side of the fireplace, with the glow from the blazing pine logs softening the harsh lines of his face, there flashed through her mind the loneliness she had sensed a short while back, she murmured smilingly,

'I bought you a present.' And, leaning over to take

167

the parcel from the small table at her side, she handed it to him. 'I heard you telling Mrs. Birchan you'd broken your inkstand. . . .'

He looked up, plainly taken by surprise.

'Thank you, Gail.' He took the parcel from her outstretched hand and slowly opened it. The inkstand, an antique in cut crystal and silver, had given her great pleasure on finding it, and now there was no doubt at all that Andrew found pleasure in owning it. 'It's exquisite.' He held it in his hand a long while, swallowing now and then, his gaze unfathomable. 'Thank you, my dear; I'll find a very good use for this charming little gift.'

'I'm glad you like it.' She averted her head, hiding the flush of pleasure his words had given her. To allow him a glimpse of her feelings would most surely mar this happy moment.

Later, as they both rose to go to bed, he appeared deliberately to bar her way—not with any obvious movement, but somehow he was between her and the door as she made to leave the room after bidding him goodnight.

'Gail. . . .' He tailed off and a moment's silence fell on the room before he said, 'Thank you again for the present, Gail. It was nice of you to think of me.' Moving aside, he allowed her to pass.

'Thank you again for the present. . . .' As she mounted the stairs Gail repeated those words ... and she had the firm conviction that other words had lingered on his tongue—words he found too difficult to voice.

The following day they attended church as usual, Andrew and Robbie in their kilts and Shena in a bright green coat with matching leggings and hat, the collar of the coat being trimmed with white fur, as was the hat which fitted snugly to her face. Gail wore an expensive tweed suit and contrasting accessories. They would have made an impressive family even had Andrew not been the wealthy and respected Laird, and

168

these his wife and children. People nodded and smiled as they went in, and again when they came out. They stood around for a while, Andrew listening to one or two problems and promising to look into them. And then they were in the car again, driving home in the clear frosty air, with the sun shining down from a cloudless sky.

After lunch they went for their usual stroll, and a sense of peace and well-being came over Gail as she walked beside her husband, with Robbie and Shena racing on in front, then returning, covering twice the distance of their parents, and more.

But in the midst of this tranquillity rose the image of Morag. She had been particularly troublesome while Gail and the children had been away; this Gail had learned from Mrs. Birchan the previous evening.

'She tried to run off, but her father caught her. I'd let her go, myself, and I think he would if she weren't ill and supposed to be resting all the while.' The housekeeper had shaken her head. 'A bad one that, Mrs. MacNeill. A black heart it is she has inside her— aye, a black heart!'

Gail mused on this as she went along beside Andrew. And she also mused on what Beth had said about Morag always remaining a barrier to Gail's happiness. And as the thought became reflected in her shadowing gaze her husband happened to glance down, apparently with some casual remark on his lips, but instead of voicing it he frowned and asked her what was wrong.

'Wrong?' she echoed uncomprehendingly.

'You're not happy.'

She started. 'What makes you say that?'

'Your expression ... it's sad.'

'I'm not sad.' Gail forced a laugh and added, 'I haven't anything to be sad about?'

'Perhaps that was too strong a word.' A pause, thoughtful and long. 'Are you unhappy, Gail?'

Why should he be questioning her like this? It was

altogether too personal for Gail and she resorted to evasion by a query of her own.

'Is anyone ever perfectly happy in this life?'

'I never said anything about perfection. It's an indeterminate state where human emotions are concerned. Human emotions involve degrees and comparisons when assessing their height or strength; with perfection there are no degrees or comparisons.' Having no wish to delve so deeply, Gail remained wrapped in silence and he added, startling her by his abruptness, 'Have you any regrets, Gail?'

'About our marriage?' She raised her eyes, seeing only him, so tall and strong beside her, so good-looking and masculine. She was unaware that the slanting sun was losing warmth with distance, or that a herd of deer was grazing on a high knoll, making a delightful silhouette against the sky. She did not realize the children were no longer running about, and making a noise, but were sitting on a pile of rocks, waiting for their parents to catch them up. 'No,' she murmured at last. 'I have no regrets.'

'There's nothing you'd have changed? *Nothing?*' How strange he sounded, she thought, and he had slackened his pace so that both he and she were scarcely moving at all. How did he want her to answer him? He seemed so tense, as if his whole fate depended on the reply she would give him. And suddenly she thought she understood. He was afraid she might be dissatisfied with her life here. Perhaps he was anxious that it might not have come up to her expectations, or that it was too quiet for her. Yes, that was what troubled him. But he must not be troubled; he had far too much already on his mind.

'No, Andrew——' She looked up and smiled at him. 'There's nothing I'd have changed.'

'Oh, but I would—I *would!*' her heart cried. 'I would have our relationship changed—I would have you love me.'

He stopped, and it seemed to Gail that a great and shuddering sigh escaped him.

'And you would never leave me?' Again she was startled by his question, but what really held her attention was the little touch of greyness appearing at the sides of his mouth. He seemed to be held in the grip of uncertainty and ... could it possibly be fear?

'I would never leave you.' She thought fleetingly of that moment when the idea actually did come to her. 'No, I'd never leave you, Andrew. Why should I?'

Ignoring her question, he said, still standing close, and looking down into her face, searchingly,

'Not even when the children grow up? Not when they're married and gone from here?'

Tightly she closed her eyes. When the children were married and gone.... What would there be for her then? An automatic existence, an unreal and undefinable position of neither wife nor servant—just someone who lived at Dunlochrie House, someone who accompanied the laird when it was desirable that he be accompanied, someone who would act as hostess to his guests and turn on the charm because that was what would be expected of her. Could she go on living a life like that, loving Andrew as she did? But by then her love might have weakened with age, or even died—untended through the years. An impatient sound issued from her husband's lips—a sign that he desired an answer, and she said,

'It's impossible to know what one's feelings will be so many years from now.'

His lips compressed.

'I told you the marriage would be binding.' An inexorable quality in his voice now and the familiar hardness in his blue eyes. His changed mood hurt, but she could find no way of guiding him back to his former almost gentle manner and she remained silent. Andrew spoke again, and the words seemed to be drawn from him against his will, voiced in tones contrasting sharply with his former inflexible reminder that the marriage would be binding, voiced in tones reflecting that same uncertainty she had noticed a few moments ago. 'As you feel now, you believe there is a possibility of your leaving me?'

Again she closed her eyes. He looked so hopeless and despairing in spite of the hardness of his features, that she could scarcely refrain from touching him, and asking him what was the matter. It was not possible, because they weren't close enough for questions such as that, but she could say, with a look of candour and sincerity in her eyes,

'As I feel now, there is no possibility of my leaving you.'

He drew a deep breath, and his step was light as they resumed their walk. His pace was also too fast for her and she began trotting to keep up with him.

'Am I walking too quickly for you?' He slowed down, his glance straying fleetingly to the hand swinging at her side.

She gained the impression that he would have liked to clasp it in his own.

On Thursday Andrew had to go away, his presence being required at one of the factories in which he had interests. The factory was in the Midlands, and he would be there for several days.

'Watch Morag,' he warned. 'I know you have to go out, but Mrs. Birchan will be on guard then. I've also arranged for the nurse to come in for several hours a day——' He broke off, shrugging. 'There's not much else I can do, apart from going to the extreme lengths of locking her in her room—in which case she'd work heself up into the kind of excitement we're all trying to avoid.' The doubt in his voice betrayed his deep anxiety that Morag might manage to leave the house in his absence and this brought from Gail a swift entreaty that he would not hold her to blame should Morag succeed in making an escape. He smiled at her. 'No, Gail, I shan't blame you.'

'I'm afraid, Andrew. Can she possibly be watched all the time?'

He shook his head.

'It's a risk I must take, Gail. I've forfeited my sport—and many other things. But I shall not neglect my business. What does one do with so wilful a girl?—beat her?' He shook his head. 'I shall not allow her to force on me such self-degradation. Morag has been my cross for many years past, and I expect she'll be my cross for many years to come, but I'm reaching the end of my patience. I don't want her to go off because her health could suffer in consequence, but I'm not willing to stand guard over her for twenty-four hours of every day.'

Never before had he spoken to her quite like this; Gail felt happy that he should do so now and she was emboldened to say,

'You've done everything you could, Andrew. You've nothing to reproach yourself for, nothing at all.'

For a moment he looked strangely at her, as if searching for a pointer to her thoughts.

'No, Gail,' he agreed at last, and the bitterness in his voice was terrible to hear. 'I have nothing to reproach myself for.'

But there was no bitterness in his voice when, about to drive off in the big car, Andrew lowered the window and said to Gail, who was standing there on the forecourt,

'Take care of yourself, my dear. Goodbye.' He smiled and gave a small salute with his hand, but Gail scarcely noticed these things, for her mind was wholly occupied with what he'd just said, and she was wondering if the slight stress placed on the 'yourself' was made by accident or design.

Morag's taunts and jeers were very much in evidence that day, but mingled with them were subtle threats.

'I'll get away somehow, and he'll blame you!'

'We've discussed this,' Gail couldn't help saying. 'And your father assured me I'll not be blamed.'

'So you talk about me behind my back, do you?'

'Not normally. But I did want to make sure I should

not be held responsible for you while your father is away.'

'Playing safe?' Morag gave a harsh laugh. 'Still trying to get round him. What's the matter? Is the celibate state tearing at your nerves?' Sick with disgust, Gail turned away. The nurse was at her lunch, but it was almost time for her to come back. Gail wasted no time when she did so, and as she was closing the door behind her she heard Morag say,

'Hello, warder number two! Never leave me a moment, do you? But I'll beat you all yet—just wait and see!'

Gail went along to the kitchen and spoke to Mrs. Birchan.

'She can't run away,' asserted the housekeeper after Gail had repeated what she had just overheard. 'Mr. MacNeil told Sinclair to keep the runabout over at his own place for the time being, because Miss Morag knows how to start it without a key. As the only other car is yours, she can't get away—so long as you make sure you don't leave the key about, that is.'

'I shan't do that,' returned Gail grimly, and then, 'She's gone away before without a car.'

'She had money for taxis, and train fares. Her father's made sure she has no money. She gave him a terrible time this morning, when you were out, taking the children to school, but he wouldn't let her have one penny.'

Gail sighed.

'How silly she is! Won't she ever learn?'

Mrs. Birchan had been rolling pastry, but she left it and washed her hands at the sink. Then she dried them on a towel, talking as she did so. 'No, Mrs. MacNeill, she won't ever learn because, for one thing, she's nothing up here to learn with.' Mrs. Birchan tapped her forehead with her hand. 'It was an evil day when Black Morag was born in this house—yes, don't look so startled, Mrs. MacNeill, that's what they call her down in the village.' She threw the towel on to the

174

table. 'An evil day for the master—but he was so proud of the babe. Aye, he was young, you see, and I remember saying about the brightness of his eyes, and the wonderment in them, if you know what I mean? It was as if he had seen a miracle. He was a soft young man in those days, with a heart as big as a football....' The woman tailed off reminiscently and silence fell for a moment or two. 'And now I sometimes wonder if he has a heart at all, so much has been done to him by Black Morag and her mother.'

Mrs. Birchan stopped, and took up the rolling pin again. 'I shouldn't be saying these things to you, but I was carried away. I did say once before that I'd let her go, if the choice were mine, and if she comes to harm then it's her own fault.'

'Well, we can't let her go, Mrs. Birchan. She must be carefully watched, for her own sake. I'm anxious, even though my husband has taken all the precautions possible.'

'The nurse is with her, I suppose?'

Gail nodded.

'She is now, but she goes off duty at six o'clock.'

'Everything will be all right. We're all about during the evening, and she won't go at night. Besides, as I've said, she hasn't any transport or any money. You can't get far without those,' Mrs. Birchan added with a reassuring smile. But she added, 'Perhaps you should lock your car in one of the garages instead of leaving it parked on the front. It is just possible that she has a key that fits.'

'Yes, I'll lock the car away when it's not in use.'

Gail then dismissed the matter of Morag and her threats to leave. As Mrs. Birchan had said, it was impossible for the girl to get far without either money or transport.

But it had never entered any of their heads that Morag might receive assistance from outside. . . .

'She must have arranged it all by phone,' said Mrs. Birchan grimly when, the following morning, it was discovered that the girl had gone. 'I thought I heard a car door close, but when I got up there was no sign of a light. I think they got away without switching the engine on; it's downhill after you're off the forecourt—all the way to the road.'

'I'll ring my husband——' She turned. 'Oh, Sinclair, there you are; I was looking for you. Would you please take Robbie and Shena to school?'

'Of course, Mrs. MacNeill.' He gave her a sympathetic glance before his eyes flickered to the housekeeper, whose red face betrayed her anger. 'Are they ready?' he inquired of Gail, and she nodded.

'They're in the car.' She looked at him. 'Thank you very much. I hope it isn't inconveniencing you at all?' she added, knowing how busy he was. He never grumbled, and Gail had very early discovered his great respect and admiration for his employer.

'It's not inconveniencing me in the least,' he replied, adding after a pause, 'If there's anything else I can do. . . ?'

'There might be, but I'll see later.'

Andrew had given her two telephone numbers: that of his hotel and that of the factory where he would be during the day. She received the same reply from both. He was not there.

'I'll ring again later,' she told Mrs. Birchan. But Gail could not rest and she went up to Morag's room and began searching around without having the slightest idea for what she was searching.

On a pad by the telephone she noticed some scribbling—idly done while Morag was speaking, Gail concluded, absently flicking back the page. More scribbling . . . but an address this time as well. Gail frowned. This was an address in Scotland. . . .

'The master's estate in Ross and Cromarty—where he goes for the stag hunting,' said Mrs. Birchan, and Gail's face fell. 'She won't be there.'

'No, of course she won't.' A small hesitation and then, as Gail tried to visualize the circumstances under which that address was written down, 'She was talking on the phone when she wrote it—and it was scribbled, just like all the other bits of things she'd been absently writing down. Is there a staff at my husband's shooting lodge?' Her colour rose slightly at having to question the housekeeper about this, but Mrs. Birchan did not reveal any surprise she might have felt.

'Only when the master's there. He has an elderly couple who live some distance away. They look to the place when he's not there and move in when he is. You see, he's only there for the shooting and it's not worth keeping a staff. The estate workers all live in their own houses, and so does the factor.'

No one there....

'How far is it, Mrs. Birchan?'

The housekeeper looked up. 'You're not going?'

'Yes, I am. Something tells me I should——'

'Miss Morag wouldn't go to a lonely place like that. It's night life she likes, not being buried in the country. As for the distance—no, it's too far to drive, if that's what you're contemplating.'

'One can drive anywhere if there are roads to drive along,' Gail replied and, after another unsuccessful attempt to contact Andrew, she decided to act immediately, no amount of argument or advice deterring her, not even Sinclair's grave warning of imminent bad weather. She gave the housekeeper instructions about the children, received Sinclair's promise that he would take them to school and bring them home again, and also that he would keep trying until he contacted Andrew, and then she set out under a darkening sky that became blacker and more threatening with every mile she travelled until, by teatime, the snow was continually building up against the windscreen, necessitating her getting out of the car in order to clear it. This happened every few minutes and her clothes were becoming soaked, clinging to her body as she drove along at a crawl, almost blinded by the massive snowflakes swirling in the headlights' glare.

Would Sinclair have been in touch with Andrew yet? she wondered, stopping once again to clear snow from the windscreen. There was a blizzard raging now, and the wind lashed at her face and legs as she proceeded with her task. How dark it was, this grim and deserted land!—and how quiet when for a few seconds the wind abated. Just the muted purr of the engine—sounding almost as if it were ready to stop—— Stop! Suddenly alarmed that this might happen, she got into the car again, relieved to hear the engine pick up at the pressure of her foot on the accelerator.

But driving was becoming difficult, and she was forced to proceed even more slowly. Dared she stop and look at the map? Had she very far to go? Was it imagination or was the snow turning to sleet? Yes, it *was* turning to sleet. Her heart lightening at this discovery, she stopped and switched on the inside light to take a look at the map. There wasn't really very far to go. . . .

It had been a long and arduous journey and the first faint glimmer of dawn was appearing over the mountains as she drove up to the lodge and peered up at the windows. No sign of life. Had she made that journey for nothing? And how would she get back if the sleet turned to snow again? The roads would be impassable. Would Andrew be furious at her impulsive action?

The car slid to a standstill and as she got out Gail noticed the bumper of another car just discernible at the corner of the building. She went towards it; a sort of lean-to afforded it some shelter and she saw that it was very old and battered. Another similar car stood a little distance away, this one covered with snow, but somehow giving the impression that it was in no better condition than the first.

Gail walked round and found the back door. To her surprise it gave to her touch and she entered this house of her husband's for the first time. Dust-sheets everywhere—how cold and deserted! But on opening the door of the drawing-room she knew instantly that someone was in residence. Dead ashes of a log fire in the hearth; bottles and glasses on the table and the arms of chairs; a record player on the table and records on the chairs and on the floor. At one end of the room the carpet had been rolled back. . . .

'Who the devil are you!' A light snapped on and Gail swung round, her heart leaping right up into her throat.

'You startled me,' she flashed angrily. 'And it's I who should be asking who you are!'

The youth was in a dressing-gown and he looked as if he'd been up all night. His eyes flicked over Gail's soaked clothing before his gaze settled on her face.

'My name's Paul. Say, you're not bad. How did you get here? Dave said another dame was coming—but no, you're too old.'

'Where,' demanded Gail icily, 'is my stepdaughter?'

'Your——?' He gaped. 'You're Morag's old man's wife? But how did you know she was here? She swore she hadn't told a soul, otherwise we'd never have come.' He stopped, his facing turning a sickly yellow colour. 'Her dad—is he here as well?' His gaze went to the window, as if he expected Morag's father to be peering in at him.

'He shouldn't be long.' Gail had no qualms about the lie, though she did not enlarge on the information she had given, but merely asked again where Morag was.

'In bed—where do you expect her to be at this time of the morning? I'd be in bed myself if I didn't have a headache. I came down to get a drink, but I won't bother. I'm getting out of this before her dad arrives. Morag's in the bedroom at the top of the stairs,' he added. 'She spoilt the party last night because she was ill. Carol had to put her to bed at eight o'clock and we've not seen her since——'

'Not . . . seen her?' faltered Gail, fear threatening to block her throat. 'Did no one go to her—later, I mean?'

He shrugged. 'We were having a party—and forgot.'

'Forgot there was someone ill in bed?' She could not

179

take that in, but she wasted no more time and a few seconds later she was with Morag, her fears increasing as she noted at once the girl's blue lips and heaving chest.

'You ... ?' Morag spoke with difficulty. 'How did you get here?' And, before Gail could answer, 'A drink, for God's sake, get me a drink!'

As she came from the bedroom Gail heard the babble of voices from another room further along the corridor.

'—I don't believe you——'

'The woman said he won't be long. Please yourself if you want to stay—but I'm moving, right now!' Gail heard no more, for by this time she had reached the bottom of the stairs. Not long afterwards, as she was sitting on the bed, holding the cup to Morag's lips, Gail heard footsteps passing the door. Someone shouted, ' 'Bye, Morag' and then the two cars were moving away, crunching over the frozen snow beneath the window.

'I must leave you for a few minutes,' said Gail to Morag as she laid her gently down again. 'I've some telephoning to do, but I'll be as quick as I can.'

Sinclair had given her the number of Andrew's factor and from him Gail received the number of a doctor. Barclay, the factor, arrived within half an hour of her telephoning him, a tall, rugged-faced man in his forties. He listened with a grave expression to what Gail had to say, shaking his head occasionally with impatience or disgust.

'Mr. MacNeill's had something to put up with; but she's never brought her friends here before.'

The reason, Gail learned presently, was that none of the young people had much money.

'They all brought food from home,' Morag said, even though Gail urged her to rest, and not to talk. 'And I raided our deep-freeze. As for the drinks ... Father always keeps plenty here, because of the shooting parties, even though he doesn't take much himself.'

'Don't talk,' said Gail again. 'Is the pain very bad?'

180

'Awful. I hope that doctor brings something with him.' She paused, breathing heavily. 'They all went without coming in to see me. I wish I hadn't invited them; and to think, I let them shoot——'

'Shoot? What did they shoot?'

'Stags—at least, that's what the three boys took the guns for. But they weren't good enough shots. Dave hit one, but it ran off before he could kill it.'

'You mean—it's injured, and—and roaming about, in this weather?'

'It'll die eventually, because if it's badly hurt it won't be able to get food.' In spite of her pain Morag managed to laugh at Gail's expression. 'What a softie you are! It's only an animal.'

Rising, Gail left the room. She found Barclay in the hall examining a gun he had found lying on the floor of the front porch. Gail imparted her news even as Barclay was about to say that the gun had been recently used.

'A wounded stag? I'll get Robertson right away; he's Mr. MacNeill's head stalker here. . . .'

Gail sat huddled up by the fire, staring into the flames, numbed in mind and body. Hours went by; now and again she leant forward and threw a few logs on to the fire, her eyes aching with sleep denied. Dawn was breaking when yet again she went over to the window and drew aside the heavy velvet curtain. A white and terrifying world ... and her husband out there, with Robertson, stalking that poor animal in order to put it out of its misery. For it was in misery; it had been seen, Robertson was told, dragging a useless leg behind it and emitting spine-chilling cries as pain and hunger overwhelmed it.

Drawing the curtain across again, Gail returned to her seat by the fire, absorbing herself in thought in order to keep awake.

So much had happened in so short a time. That nerve-racking drive in the ambulance, with the vehicle skidding and swerving down the narrow winding lane; and then the relief as the main road was reached and some sort of speed could be maintained.

But it had all been in vain. Twenty minutes after being admitted to hospital Morag was dead. The doctor coming to Gail in the chill bleak waiting-room ... the nightmare drive home in a taxi ... the utter weariness and dejection. Gail knew she would never forget this night as long as she lived. For on reaching the lodge she had learned that Andrew had arrived just a few minutes ago and, having been informed of Morag's death by Barclay and deciding he could gain nothing by going to the hospital, he went out with Robertson to search for the wounded stag.

All night long they had been out. The sleet had turned to snow again, as Gail surmised it would, but by the time she arrived back from the hospital it had stopped and a full moon shone from a clear sky. But a sky like that portended a severe frost and Gail shivered with fear as much as cold each time she left the fire and went to the window. Andrew out there, searching and stalking ... crawling on his stomach, edging closer and closer so as to be able to aim at the head or the neck. The stag, alert because of its hunger and pain, would sense the presence of its adversaries and keep moving on, to become lost to view. Robertson would sight it again and the whole wearying process would be repeated, the men dropping once more to their stomachs, slithering through the snow, their clothing sodden and freezing on their shivering bodies. Gail knew her husband could kill at a distance of two hundred yards, but she somehow felt that in this instance he would get closer, much closer, for the animal must be dispatched with one painless shot. Andrew would make doubly sure of this.

How long would that take? But they would not be home until that unfortunate stag was secured, and Gail herself would not have it otherwise—but the fear for Andrew was great, so great that it hurt. Would he contact pneumonia—or something even worse? Rheumatic fever...?

She stood up again, wringing her hands, and the next moment she was back in her chair. Think of something else. Morag—— No, not Morag!

Someone was moving about in the kitchen. Mrs. Irvine and her husband, preparing to light the fires, and get the boiler going, and the breakfast.

Mr. and Mrs. Irvine were the couple employed by Andrew to keep an eye on the lodge; they had been there when Gail arrived back from the hospital, having been sent for by Barclay. They had tidied up the mess in the sitting-room and lighted a fire. The whole room had been transformed in Gail's absence, and elsewhere in the house dust covers had come off and fires had been lighted in the bedrooms.

'It's to your bed you're going,' the woman had declared with all the aggressiveness of her Scottish forebears. 'You're looking all in, and I've heard about you driving through the night, and then sitting with Miss Morag for hours waiting for the ambulance.' Mrs. Irvine had scrutinized Gail for a long moment, her tongue clicking as she did so. 'I've aired the mattress and there's a lovely fire in your room. I'm away to make up the bed and I'll call you when it's done.'

'I'm waiting until my husband gets back——'

'Why must you wait for him?' demanded Mrs. Irvine pugnaciously. 'He'll not be back this night, unless I'm very much mistaken.'

'I won't sleep with him being out there. I—I want to wait to see if he's all right.'

'All right? Of course he'll be all right. Now just you come up when I call—and no more of this nonsense!'

Too weary for further argument, Gail went meekly upstairs and adopted an air of resignation until the departure of the old woman from the room. Half an hour later on hearing the couple go to bed, Gail crept downstairs and into the sitting-room, where she had been ever since.

Mrs. Irvine's footsteps could now be heard coming along the hall; she opened the door, a bucket and shovel in her hand.

'What——?' The woman stared at Gail, sitting there, fully dressed, before a fire clogged up with dead ash. 'Mrs. MacNeill!' she exclaimed admonishingly. 'You never went to bed!'

'No; I'm sorry, but I wouldn't have slept, not with my husband in danger—— Oh, Mrs. Irvine,' she cried distractedly, 'whatever can have happened to them? Do you think they could have fallen in a loch?'

'Fallen——?' Mrs. Irvine blinked at her. 'Now what would they be wanting to fall in a loch for?'

'If the loch was covered with ice and snow they couldn't see it....' She tailed off, staring as if she had seen a ghost. Andrew stood in the doorway, soaked to the skin and caked in mud and grime, a rank-smelling vegetation adhering to his clothing and his hair.

'Andrew ... you're safe!' Gail took a few faltering steps towards him, the scar livid against the pallor of her skin. 'You're safe——' Her legs went from under her, but Andrew caught her before she fell.

'Darling——' Gently he laid her down on the couch and she managed a wan little smile. 'Darling, you're all in. Why aren't you in bed?'

Her eyelids became heavy and fluttered down; she tried to speak, but her nerves were all to pieces and she just shook her head feebly.

'I told her you'd be all right, sir,' Mrs. Irvine began. 'And I also said she must go to bed—two nights she's been away from her bed! But she said she wouldn't sleep, with you being out there—seemed to think you were in some sort of danger.'

Gail's eyes opened; Andrew's arm slid under her shoulders and she was eased up. He held a glass to her lips; she drank from it and smiled again. Had she dreamt it, or had he really called her darling? There was no doubt about the tenderness in his eyes now—and he was looking at her with an odd perception too, as if he had made a sudden discovery.

'Andrew,' she breathed as he put her back against the cushions. 'You—called m-me—called me——'

'Mrs. Irvine,' he said, turning to the old woman who was preparing to leave them alone, 'is the bed ready?'

'I'll warm it again, sir, and light a fire.'

'Thank you; be as quick as you can, I don't want Mrs. MacNeill to fall asleep here.'

'I don't want to go to bed.' Gail tried to rise, but a hand on her shoulder kept her where she was. 'I'm not going,' she said more firmly as the door closed behind Mrs. Irvine.

'Not going?' frowned Andrew. 'Why?'

'You called me darling——'

His mouth curved with amusement.

'Is that any reason for your not going to bed?'

She blushed, feeling foolish as he continued to stare down at her, the humorous curve still on his lips. 'You're soaked,' she managed to say at last. 'You must go and change, and have a bath.' Her eyelids drooped and she could scarcely keep awake.

'Gail,' he said sharply, 'don't go to sleep here.'

But although she fought against it, sleep overtook her and her husband left her there on the couch, merely tucking a rug around her and drawing the curtains so that the room was in darkness except for the glow from the fire.

She awoke partly refreshed but still tired. Someone had been in and attended to the fire, but the warmth that enveloped Gail came from another source altogether. Andrew loved her. . . .

'You're awake, Mrs. MacNeill.' From the quietness of the hall Mrs. Irvine appeared, her eyes keen and searching. 'Feeling better for your sleep?'

Gail nodded.

'My husband—is he all right?'

'All right? But of course he's all right. He's been sleeping, but he's up now; I heard him a few minutes ago. Would you like a nice cup of tea?'

'In a little while. I want a bath first.' She had packed a suitcase with underwear and night clothes, but Mrs. Birchan had insisted on putting in a couple of dresses and for this Gail was thankful, having spent over forty-eight hours in the dress she now wore.

Mrs. Irvine threw a massive log on the fire.

'You go and have your bath,' she said, turning to Gail, 'and I'll have a pot of tea ready when you come down. I have a dinner cooking, but you'll not be wanting it yet awhile—not with just getting up.'

'What time is it?' asked Gail curiously.

'Almost seven o'clock. Both you and the master have been asleep for the whole day.'

When Gail came down, much refreshed after her bath and change of clothing, Andrew was standing with his back to the fire, clad in a dressing-gown and yet appearing almost immaculate—so clean and cool and showing no sign of having suffered in any way from his experience out there in the snowy wastes. But there was a certain grimness about him which portrayed the fact that the tragedy of Morag had been very much on his mind, and indeed, it still was. But it was Gail who spoke of her, saying with deep regret,

'Morag ... there was no hope, Andrew. I arrived too late. And when the ambulance finally did come its progress was so so slow until we reached the main road. I'm so sorry, Andrew.'

Silence dropped on the room, but after a little while Andrew spoke, and his tones, unlike those of Gail, were devoid of emotion.

'You did all you could, my dear, and I thank you.' His eyes met hers and she saw them darken with sudden tenderness and love. 'You were wonderful; I heard it all from Sinclair and Barclay and Mrs. Irvine.' He fell silent again as she lowered her head, hiding her face, for her colour had risen at his praise. 'I have things to do for Morag,' he continued in the same unemotional tones. 'And they will be done, of course.

186

But after that we shall not mention her again.' Leaning forward, he tilted up her face with a finger under her chin. 'You understand, Gail? I do not want her name mentioned again.'

She swallowed and a pained expression crossed her face. But she nodded and said, almost inaudibly,

'Yes, Andrew, I understand.'

He looked at her hard and long before releasing her.

'I think you do understand,' he murmured. 'I believe you understand everything.'

She inclined her head. He was absolutely sure, then, that Morag was not his. And he obviously felt convinced that Gail had also guessed at the truth.

They both looked up as Mrs. Irvine entered with the tea tray and set it down on a table by the fire.

'Will you be eating, sir?' she inquired. 'I have a dinner in the oven.'

'We shall probably eat later.' He glanced at Gail. 'Unless you're hungry now?'

She shook her head. 'I couldn't eat anything at present.'

When Mrs. Irvine had gone, and they were drinking their tea, Andrew spoke to Gail more intimately than ever before. He had early begun to suspect that Morag was not his, but when left with her he had tried to forget this and had given her a father's affection and care. As for his wife, he took her back, but could not forgive her.

'She went away again and I tormented myself that I was partly to blame. I felt a hypocrite—going to church on Sunday and yet not practising the Christian creed of forgiveness. So the next time she came back we had Robbie and Shena——'

'You were willing to make a completely new start?' Gail recalled her sister's assertion that Andrew was a good man and would consider marriage to be permanent. But Andrew was shaking his head, although a little sadly.

'I tried, Gail, but it wasn't possible to forget, and in

187

order to forgive one must forget what one has suffered. It didn't help when Morag turned out the way she did. I truly believed she was to be my permanent cross in this life.'

His face was drawn, but as Gail looked at him with tender compassion his smile appeared and, removing the table, he sat down next to her on the couch. His arm went around her and she nestled close, resting her head against his breast.

'You mustn't blame yourself, Andrew,' she whispered. 'It's very hard, sometimes, to forgive.' She was thinking of Michael and the wrong he did her, but Andrew was kissing her and she could not tell him about that for quite a time.

'My dear sweet wife,' he murmured, his lips caressing her cheek. 'Darling, when I asked you if there was anything you would have changed—did you love me then?'

She nodded.

'Yes, Andrew.' She leant away, her glance searching as the import of the question struck her. 'You loved me at that time?'

'I loved you, Gail, and I did so want you to give me some indication that my love was returned. That's why I asked the question.' He kissed her tenderly, as if by so doing he could erase the memory of his disappointment on receiving her firm reply that there was nothing she would have changed.

'How silly I was,' she said musingly. 'I quite misunderstood you, Andrew.'

'It doesn't matter now, my love.' Her hair was a little tousled, as well it might be, and the scar was revealed. Andrew touched it with his lips. 'I love you so, my Gail—my beautiful wife.'

For a long while she remained silent, and then she drew away from his embrace and stood up, turning her back to him as she gazed into the fire.

'Andrew. . . .'

'Sweetheart?' Surprise in his tone, and a hint of puzzlement.

'You've told me everything, and now I have something to tell you.' She clasped her hands tightly, as if the action would give her the strength to continue as she went on to tell Andrew about Michael and the accident, and the scars on her body. She told him that Michael had been the cause of the accident, having had too much to drink. And she left the most difficult thing she had to say until the last. 'The real reason why he broke the engagement was because—because I received internal injuries....' A profound silence followed and she turned to face him, her beautiful eyes wide and a little afraid. 'Andrew, do you mind that we can never have children?'

Another silence, and then she was in his arms, her head on his breast again as they stood together by the fire. He expressed deep remorse for his suspicions, but Gail pressed a finger to his lips and spoke herself, telling him she intended entering hospital to have something done about the scars.

'I can't bear to let you go, my darling,' he began, when she interrupted him.

'It won't be for long, Andrew. I don't want to be away from you and the children, but——' She glanced pleadingly at him. 'I'll feel much happier without the scars.'

'Then it shall be as you wish, sweetheart, although I shall hate every moment you're away from me.' He held her very close and as the thought struck him he told her he had decided not to allow the children's grandmother to see them again. He had learned from Robbie how they disliked her and he did not see why they should be made unhappy by her visits. At his mention of Robbie she said again,

'You don't mind that we can't have children?'

He bent and kissed her, with infinite tenderness.

'Darling,' he said softly, 'we have two children—one of each kind. I don't really think we need any more, do you?' His voice was edged with tender humour that brought an instant smile to her lips.

'No,' she returned, shaking her head. 'I don't really think we need any more.'

Harlequin Presents..

Some of the world's greatest romance authors.
Don't miss any of this exciting series.

- [ ] 67 ACCOMPANIED BY HIS WIFE, Mary Burchell
- [ ] 68 AND THEN CAME LOVE, Roberta Leigh
- [ ] 69 MASTER OF FALCON'S HEAD, Anne Mather
- [ ] 70 THE CHATEAU OF ST. AVRELL, Violet Winspear
- [ ] 71 AND NO REGRETS, Rosalind Brett
- [ ] 72 THE WAY OF A TYRANT, Anne Hampson
- [ ] 73 FOOD FOR LOVE, Rachel Lindsay
- [ ] 74 LEOPARD IN THE SNOW, Anne Mather
- [ ] 75 DARE I BE HAPPY?, Mary Burchell
- [ ] 76 HEART OF THE LION, Roberta Leigh
- [ ] 77 THE JAPANESE SCREEN, Anne Mather
- [ ] 78 A MAN LIKE DAINTREE, Margaret Way

PLEASE NOTE: All Harlequin Presents novels from #83 onwards are 95c. Books below that number, **where available** are priced at 75c through Harlequin Reader Service until December 31st, 1975.

Some of the world's greatest romance authors.
Don't miss any of this exciting series.

These titles are available at your local bookseller, or through the Harlequin Reader Service, M.P.O. Box 707, Niagara Falls, N.Y. 14302; Canadian address 649 Ontario St., Stratford, Ont.

H